Outer Limits
Hidden Lives

Hillingdon Literary Festival

2018 Community Creative Writing Anthology

Brunel Centre for Contemporary Writing

Championing the diverse voices of the London Borough of Hillingdon

Published in 2018 by

Hillingdon Literary Festival
Brunel University London
Kingston Lane
Uxbridge
Middlesex
UB8 3PH
United Kingdom

www.HillingdonLiteraryFestival.com

© All rights reserved
The Copyright of each contribution rests with the individual artist and authors and no part of this publication may be reproduced, stored in a retrieval system or transmitted in any form or by any means without the prior written permission of the individual artist or author.

BRITISH LIBRARY
CATALOGUING-IN-PUBLICATION DATA
A full record of this book is available from the British Library

ISBN 978-1-9085494-2-6

Printed and bound in the UK by
Minuteman Press Uxbridge

Contents

Welcome – Professor William Leahy	1
Foreword – Professor Philip Tew	3
Introduction – Sebastian Jenner	4

John Donegan 6
A Pasteurised Brickwork Quilt

James F McDermot 8
The Years Go By

Sola Janet Browne 16
Roundhouse

Sarah Badhan 18
Kutcha Butcha

Samuel Green 29
Life in Mariana

Neil Parker 30
Party

Michelle Stevens 32
The Graduate Matthew Pierce

Jonathan Pizarro 42
Fuchsine

Hilary Lynch 44
The Poll Tax Demonstration

Angela Narayn 57
Images of Eastbourne

Chris Miller 61
The Thing About Geoff

Jordan Friend 69
Big Boys Cry Too

Andy Lewis 72
No Offence

Vivienne Burgess 75
The Office Treehouse

Eden Kofi Joseph 86
Fear of Love

Jake Horowitz 90
Leo and Cole

Simon Engwell 94
Bridge Sighs to Soothe City Street

Russell Christie 97
The Honey Bees of Syria

Taiwo Oyenola 107
Tallaahi (I swear by God)

Matthew Healing 112
ALONELY

Macauley Raymond Foster *A Broken Deck*	113
Mark O'Loughlin *Pink Petals*	116
Lia Courtenay Harlin *How To Be A Good Spy*	118
Connor Smith *Uxbridge? Is that London?*	126
Adam Johnson *Spinning Time*	128
Vivien Brown *When The Party's Over*	133
Aisling Lally *The Sister*	134
Luke Buffini *The Pregnant Afternoon*	138
Iris Hontiveros Mauricio *Sometimes I Hear Them*	148
Lorraine Collins *The Enemy Within*	150
Christina Barnatsos *Pass and Past*	164

Welcome – Professor Bill Leahy

Vice Provost – Students, Staff and Civic Engagement Brunel University London

At Brunel University London, we are committed to promoting young and emerging talent and to playing an active part in the local community – so I am delighted that this creative writing competition, *Outer Limits : Hidden Lives* is a key part of the fourth Hillingdon Literary Festival. You can see from the entries contained in this anthology that there is no shortage of writing talent in Hillingdon.

I understand our aim in launching the competition was to provide a platform for the diverse voices here at Brunel and across the Borough – and as you can see from what follows, we have certainly achieved this!

Getting published is always a challenge for new writers and any help they can receive along the way is very welcome. I hope those included in the volume – and especially the overall winner – are very proud of their achievements.

We are – as indeed the Hillingdon Literary Festival itself shows – determined to be of and for our local community; working to build strong, mutually beneficial partnerships, but we also want to help our students and those we support in Hillingdon achieve and value excellence.

The competition and anthology would not have been possible without, on the one hand, the hard work of our judges – Suzi Feay, Daljit Nagra, and Philip Tew – and Seb Jenner, the Festival Producer, and a Brunel PhD student who has shown himself extraordinarily adept at organising numerous large scale events; and, on the other, our sponsors: the London Borough of Hillingdon, Heathrow and the Arts Council for England.

Good luck to all those whose work is contained in this volume. We look forward to reading more of your work in the near future.

Foreword – Professor Philip Tew

Director, Hillingdon Literary Festival, and, Brunel Centre for Contemporary Writing

A creative writing anthology has become a firm feature of the annual Hillingdon Literary Festival (HiLF), hosted by Brunel University London and organised by the Brunel Centre of Contemporary Writing (BCCW) in collaboration with the London Borough of Hillingdon. Those producing this current volume are delighted to draw from both parts of the community of Hillingdon that were traditionally referred to as 'town' and 'gown' (in other words, to be more contemporary, the local community *and* Brunel University that is embedded in that community).

Much as HiLF does, this anthology seeks to foster an ongoing tradition of collaboration between town and gown through the medium of literature, approached both as consumers (readers) and producers (writers) that are the key elements and lifeblood of any such festival. The BCCW aspires to act as a bridge between these two sectors, and inspire and foster a creative presence in Hillingdon that can thrive all year round. We hope ever more people will contribute creatively in future and also attend HiLF. So in such a democratic spirit of literary self-expresion and appreciation for all, please read and enjoy the poetry and prose contained in this year's publication.

Introduction – Sebastian Jenner

Festival Producer and Editor

Inspired by the extraordinary talent in our community – so apparent at each Hillingdon Literary Festival – we organise a community creative writing competition and associated anthology each year.

This year's anthology, *Outer Limits : Hidden Lives*, features stories and poems carefully selected from over two hundred submissions. Every single one of these was read with pleasure and awe, and it's a great shame that we could not print more. The talent in our Borough truly is exceptional, impressive and diverse – it's an honour to be in the position to champion it.

This collection is made freely available to the community, distributed at the festival, to all seventeen brilliant Hillingdon libraries, and online for e-book download.

We trust you'll enjoy reading the proud and brilliant voices of our community.

by Jacqueline Chesta

A Pasteurised Brickwork Quilt
by John Donegan

There's a party going on in London,
But not everyone's invited,
Its called the 24-hour tube,
Access is limited, but desirable,
to the chosen few.

I remember trying to get into a party
where I wasn't invited,
He's too much trouble, they said, I used the
famous line.
"Don't you know who I am?"
Followed by the equally preposterous
"You better know, because I'm gonna be
somebody"… Who or what that somebody was,
I'm yet to find out.

The Outer Boroughs of London are like that.
Unsure of what or who they are.
Suburban Wastelands, a gregarious
pasteurised brick work quilt,
Of neatly paraded houses, flats, developments,
planted side by side,
To the abandonment of trendy
Million-pound studios,
Lauded by The Standard and Hipster
propergandum machines.
Ignored by *Time Out*, to them London seems to
end at Acton, but starts in Hackney,

Hoxton and Brick Lane.
The 24-hour tube doesn't go as far as Eastcote,
Ruislip or end up in Uxbridge, nor anywhere in
The Borough of Hillingdon.
Disenfranchised from the rest of London, you
make up your own rules,
your own way of doing things.
This perpetually creates an increased sense of
awareness to be different,
a sense of togetherness,
A state of community.
The state of community which
leads to a creative community.
A hub of singing, dancing, music, theatre,
laughter, humour, drama, poetry, verse.

The idea that Outer London Boroughs can have a
creative community,
In the light of musical venues such as pubs
closing down at such alarming rates,
Budgets being withdrawn or reduced for drama
and theatre venues, Is a wondrous proration.

To overcome this massive obstacle, the
communities of Hillingdon are getting together,
Funding projects with help from local businesses.
Arranging committees, choosing leaders,
And organising local festivals and events leading
to a creative community.
The Creative community of
The Wonderful and Salubrious
London Borough of Hillingdon.

The Years Go By
by James F. McDermot

I'm at the checkout of the Esso Petrol Station at the Tesco Express on Cowley High Street, on my way into Uxbridge, talking about prawns.
I've walked into something. Not an argument, but certainly an intense discussion between the cashier and a young taxi driver. They turn to me and want me to resolve an issue. It seems they perceive me at once to be a fair-minded, impartial and intellectual outsider. Not a bad summary for a first impression and I admire them for their perspicacity. They want to know whether prawns are *halal* or *haram*.

"Where do prawns come from?" they ask. I tell them what I know. They are aquatic creatures, mostly from the sea, but some are fresh water, raised in farms. Can they live outside water? No, they are not amphibious. Like fish, they will die out of water.

"How are they caught?"

Most people don't realise that their natural colour is grey. The boys are suspicious of this and want reassurance. I am reminded of the diner in a Glaswegian restaurant who, seeing a prawn dish on the menu, enquires of the waitress

"How are the prawns?"

"They're wee pink fish," she replies.

I describe the trawling for prawns. Either they are frozen, or immersed in boiling water to cook them at once. The latter produces the miraculous colour change. They are convinced, but we have not solved our problem.

"What do they eat?"

I can't tell them with any certainty. The diet of any living creature destined for consumption is vital to our problem. And it gets even more complicated. What about prawn cocktail-flavoured crisps?

"I'll tell you what. I will ask my clever solicitor friend. She knows all about these things, and she is bound to have an answer. Why don't I stop by at the same time next week? I'll see what I can find out by then."

I leave them before their first impressions of me are dimmed by my ignorance.
So that's how I come to e-mail Sangeeta, and pose the question of her. Prawns? *Halal* or *Haram?* A simple question, deserving a simple answer. But nothing is simple to a lawyer.

"It all depends," she says.

I ponder what I will say to my new friends at the petrol station next week and I reflect how much the town has changed since I was here in 1965. The forgotten memories of the past tumble back into my consciousness in the present.

It's the thirtieth of April. Second term already in London and some of the old school pals, now undergraduates, have come up to Brunel for the weekend. Brunel wasn't even a university then, it didn't get its charter until the next year. There is the party, all night. The star attraction is The

Who, still spotty teenagers famous for smashing up hotel rooms and their guitars.

Before the party we go up to Stanilaus's room on the first floor in the corner of the College quad. That's where I meet Julia. Her brother is on the same course as me. She had a Spanish mother and inherited the sort of smooth olive skin and dark brown eyes that inspired Al Martino to sing:

Soon I'll return,
Bringing you all the love your heart can hold
Please say "si si"
Say you and your Spanish eyes will wait for me

But she doesn't see me. Not superiority, not arrogance, certainly not bad manners. I just don't register with her. She is simply so pretty and alive that everybody courts her attention. There are so many chaps more clever, better looking, better connected, more socially accomplished who try to impress her. How can I compete? How can I get her to notice me? I try to talk to her but I make a fool of myself.

The answer must be in the bottom of an empty jug of beer. Forget the spliffs that are being passed around on a pin to cement the common descent into loving oblivion. Where is a bar? A few drinks and I will think I will find that answer.

I don't remember much after the fifth pint. I know I got seven of us into the Ford Anglia and we drive to the reservoir near Staines. Drinking and driving? Not a problem then. In those days we celebrated passing the driving test with a pub Crawl. Anyone who took part in a house play at school can say, "the Leith police dismisseth us," without stumbling. Anyone who went through years of slip practice in the nets can touch his nose with both index fingers, sober or drunk.

We come across an old rowing boat on the edge of the lake. We find the oars hidden under the boathouse and paddle across to the man-made island. Stretching out in a state of inebriated bliss, we watch the sun burn off the whirls of mist on the lake as it rises from the east. Back on the campus by six o'clock, we throw ourselves into the May Day celebrations. Not a parade, but a spontaneous, multi-facetted celebration of a pagan feast. Morris dancers jostle with hippies. Remember also, this is the time of flower power. Saffron-clad monks with shaven heads and bare feet chant *hari Krishna*. Tobacco smoke laden with brown sugar creates a haze of well-being. "If you're going to San Francisco", sings Scott McKenzie. No, there is no need. And we've already got some flowers in our hair. It is all happening here.

Julia reminds me of an Annigoni painting that is being used to promote a perfume. I look it up, it's Cristina II. A week later I telephone the perfume company and they send me a poster-sized print. I frame it and hang it in the hall. I can't get her out of my thoughts. Boys fall in love with an image. That's not a criticism but a simple statement of fact. That's how we are, the way we are made. Call it primeval, antediluvian, atavistic, whatever. Be as rude as you like, but that's how it is. What can I do to win her? Shall I write her one of my poems? I'll think about it. Ten days later the telephone rings and I am confounded into silence. It is Julia.

"You won't remember me," she says, "But we met with Stani over the May Day weekend. I need you to do something for me. It's to do with my brother. Will you help?"
It's not straightforward. Simon is losing his way. The two of them are orphans and Julia has assumed a maternal role despite her own youth. She is protective.

"Simon is my only family now," she says. Their father died in a traffic accident when they were both young. Their mother died from cancer only a year ago. Simon hasn't coped well. He's missing lectures and tutorials.

"Will you look after him whilst I am not there? He rooms next to you. Will you make friends with him? Stani says you are a solid chap. You can be relied upon."

It flatters me that she asks but I wonder if I can help. She must know the path Simon has taken. It's clear that he is injecting himself with something. He always looks spaced out. Since I came to Brunel I have avoided the sub-culture that permeates some parts of the college. Each to his own. But I can't deny Julia.

"Leave it to me," I say. "I'll look after him."

"I will show my gratitude," she says.

She comes up to see Simon at the weekend of the Uxbridge Blues and Folk festival on the 19th June. Do you remember it? No, of course you don't, because it was probably thirty years before you were born. But I do remember, I was there. I'll tell you about it. Marianne Faithfull is one of the headline acts and she's just had a hit with "This Little Bird". I remember that it was a bob to get in. That's 5p nowadays. The Who are there as usual, straight from their residency at the Blue Moon Club in Hayes. Zoot Money's Big Roll Band, The Birds, Spencer Davis, Long John Baldry, Cliff Bennett and the Rebel Rousers, John Mayall. Anyone who mattered.

Promiscuity is an old diversion and you don't think of it as such at the time. Julia and I fell into one another's arms in that uncomplicated way that young people do.

"I know that's what you wanted," she said after we had made love. "I remember how your mournful eyes followed me everywhere over that May Day weekend."

She says that she will see me again soon. She says that she'll be up again to see Simon of four weeks' time. I can't believe how kind fate has been to me. I start to count the minutes of those long four weeks. I am in love.

Simon was found in the Grand Union Canal by Cowley Lock about ten days later. His lungs were full of water but he could have overdosed long before that. No party, no Morris dancers, and no festival this time to witness his death. Julia's dismissal of me was unforgiving and final.

"I trusted you and you let me down," said Julia. "Don't even come to his funeral."

Where did the years go? I am back where I was as a student. Since then I have built one business and then another. I've travelled to every continent, several times. I've played every racquet sport you can imagine, badly. Cricket, tennis, hockey, squash and polo. Afterwards I lost touch with Stani but kept up with his career through the financial pages of the newspapers. A successful banker. Julia, I hear you ask. It's a funny thing but I still have that Annigoni print, stored in the loft. I don't know where she is now, and that probably is a good thing. Did I see her again after the tragic circumstances of our parting? Well, yes, once, but not to speak to. About ten years after her brother died I was checking in at Terminal Three for a flight to New York. I turned to my briefcase on top of the suitcase and saw her passing by, pushing a trolley, with a pretty little girl pulling her own mini-suitcase, bright pink, with two small wheels. She was too far away to call, and I couldn't leave in the middle of checking in. I waited for my boarding card and the return of my passport and went looking for them. Smith's, Boots and the doorways of all those emporiums designed to alleviate the boredom of modern airports.

I couldn't find them. I had the merest glance of the young girl, and I started to wonder. It is possible, could she be mine? I don't know. I thought of the girl and calculated with a guess at her age. Would Julia have told me? Certainly not then, for she had promised with the single-minded determination she always showed, never to speak to me again, never to ask another favour. Mellowing with the years? Perhaps not: people are more loyal to their enemies than their friends, they keep them longer. But the young girl? Maybe. I wait now for the day, without much real hope or expectation, but just in case, when the telephone might ring or there is a knock on the door. An almost familiar voice might say: you won't remember me, just as her mother had said all those years ago.

But I've found an answer for the cashier and the taxi driver. Sangeeta has contacted her Imam and they have debated the matter in great depth. They have the definitive ruling:
prawns are *mukhru*.

Roundhouse
by Sola Janet Browne

My first house was a round house.
No four walls, just constantly curving horizons
enveloping my mass.
Folded in the folds of her middle
my DNA was still but a riddle.
Not yet fully pieced together

I miss the peace I had within her.
My mother.
My first home.
My first town centre around her centre,
her womb my first local.

My native land. The Motherland.
I wish I could go back.
They are constantly telling us to go back.

by Richard Wilde

Kutcha Butcha
by Sarah Badhan

Anglo-Indian.

I first heard the phrase uttered by my Mother. We were at the dinner table, I can't recall how the conversation came about, but that's the first time I had a name for what I was. There are many others. Half-Caste. Mixed Race. Dual-heritage. Interracial. Kutcha-Butcha.

I don't think my parents ever thought about the implications of raising children that were half white and half brown. During my childhood it was a non-issue. It was only later that it became more complicated. I certainly felt as though I had the best of both worlds growing up. Saturday morning. Round to my maternal grandparents. Activities consisted of reading books, baking cakes, eating Heinz Tomato Soup and Jacobs Cream Crackers for lunch. Saturday evening. Mum would plait mine and my sister's hair, we'd change into a Salwar Kameez, and stand on little wooden stools to "help" make Roti for dinner at my Dad's family home.

"Where are you from?"

The feeling of never being able to be 'placed'. To never be ever quite 'known'. My cappuccino skin always needing an explanation. In later years I will like being different. In an office full of the same colour skin and the same accents I will come to appreciate my point of difference.

My parents met at school when they were sixteen. I know that there was a lot sneaking around in the early days – neither side knowing how their respective families would react to the fact of their relationship. Suffice to say Britain in the 1970s wasn't exactly leading the way in fairness, equality and tolerance when it came to attitudes to other cultures and ethnicities. When my paternal grandparents found about by Mum they told my Dad that "White girls are only after one thing". On my Mum's side, her Dad tried to gently explain to my her that even if the relationship succeeded she should think about the implications of raising children that were "Neither one thing nor the other" and how "Confusing" it would be. Frankly, given the resistance they both faced it's amazing I'm here at all.

In stories, Grandfather always described the family house in New Delhi as a palace. Three storeys tall, so many bedrooms you would get lost wandering around, a gigantic roof big enough for playing badminton as well as sleeping under the stars. We would hear how we'd have servants waiting on us, ready to attend to our every need. It was the stuff of dreams.

By the time I reached India a decade after these stories were told, the once gleaming marble house had fallen into disrepair. A layer of dust covered every surface. Furniture was disintegrating, now largely unusable. I sat on the roof, barren apart from dirt and rubble, and imagined my Dad and his brothers twenty years ago – having water fights and eating meals. The good times are fleeting.

"Sat Sri Akal".

That's the limit of my Punjabi. The relatives I meet are frustrated to learn that I'm not able to converse with them; that I only speak English. My Indian genes may as well not exist. I feel useless. I feel white.

The love of my Indian heritage waxes and wanes throughout childhood. In early years it's thrilling, glamorous, loud, bolshy and demanding attention. In teenage years I resent having to get dressed up and go to weddings that last three days, mixing with people I don't even know. The brashness starts to grate and, if I'm not in the right mood, it's exhausting.

My first visit to the place my Dad was born was a culture-shock to say the least. There were no road signs to direct our driver to the tiny village in the Punjab, so we were reliant on my Grandmother to navigate.

"Next left at that tree!"
"Take a right at the water pump!"
"Keeping going for three-fields along!"

We were given a warm welcome when we arrived. It felt like the whole village had turned out. I had no idea who anyone was but my Grandmother and Aunts greeted everyone in turn as though they had only seen each other last week. We were led through narrow streets to the small house where my Dad was born. It felt claustrophobic. The house itself was painted a pale blue colour with dark blue shutters. It looked to me like a 'toy-house', big enough for one or two people perhaps – but not a whole family. The courtyard out the back was bigger than the inside, and overlooked the lush green fields, giving a sense of space and freedom. This was where we all gravitated to, to have our Chai.

What struck me on this visit was how little people had. Their homes were functional – no decorations and only the most basic of furniture. I saw my Dad become emotional when an elderly lady sitting across the room for us told him how she remembered him as a small boy. This visit must have felt something like a homecoming of sorts for my Dad. Whilst I was pondering on my dual-identity, I suppose he was too. He was an Indian who was raised in Britain – who had brown skin but spoke with an English accent and supported QPR. I never supposed my Dad struggled with his identity and I never asked him, but he must have felt the same quandary I did.

My Grandmother and her sister are farmer's daughters. They are two of five girls and were raised in the bread basket of India, with the buffaloes and the peacocks. When I am around thirteen, 'Auntie' comes over from India for six months to visit. Though their features are the same, she's got a much darker complexion than my Grandmother. She's only a couple of years older than her, but her skin is tougher, coarser, and her eyes too seem harder and steely somehow. I can't help but feel sorry that she has had to endure so many years of rural Indian life, whilst my Grandmother escaped to raise six children in a semi-detached house in West London. This sense of "what could have been", knowing what life for people can be like on the other side of the world, guides me through life – and makes me eternally grateful for what I have and where I am.

We want to show her what the UK looks like so we take her to Windsor Castle, Big Ben, Buckingham Palace, the London Eye. She poses proudly in front of all these landmarks.
I always wondered what Auntie made of her time in the UK. I wonder if it felt cold and inhospitable to her, isolating even. London, even our part of West London, is a big and lonely place at times. I wonder whether she missed her community at home. Despite our various outings to see the sights, the cold British weather meant she was stuck indoors a lot of the time which she would have found tough after spending a life outside in the sunshine in the village back home. I viewed my Grandmother differently after her sister's visit. I felt proud of her for doing a hard thing in leaving her family in the Punjab back in the 1960s to start a new life overseas – not knowing anything about the culture, or how

things would work out. That decision taken by my Grandparents to leave their Motherland led to my Dad being raised as British-Indian and meeting my Mother in the suburbs of West London at the local comp. How different things might have been.

My suitcase is packed full of outfits, complete with matching bindis, bangles, earrings and shoes. Not one, but two, of my Uncles are getting married. In India. To two women they have never met before. No one is using the term "arranged marriage" but as far as I'm concerned, that is what it is. I suppose the more trendy name would be "assisted marriage". Perhaps that softens the blow and makes it more socially acceptable. "Arranged marriage" implies coercion, force, lack of free-will. My Uncles have entered into it willingly. The first Uncle is divorced and there is pressure on him to marry again. The second is nearing forty and feels he should settle down. Yes, there is pressure from my Grandmother but it's their decision to go through with it. I hope their wives-to-be also had a choice but in reality I don't know. So here we are heading off to India for a double wedding celebration.

The whole thing is fucked up. It doesn't sit well with me. I'm outraged by it. I always thought I was from a progressive, forward-thinking family – one that celebrated difference. I am the product of that after all. It feels wrong and backwards, though everyone else just accepts is as tradition. My seventeen-year old self can't reconcile the fact that at school I am learning about feminism from an awe-inspiring English teacher who is encouraging me to read Margaret Atwood's *The Handmaid's Tale* and Kate Chopin's *The Awakening*, yet in my home life I am being subliminally told that marriage is the only way forward. It disturbs me so much that I start to have nightmares. A recurring one is particularly poignant. I'm chained to a bed and my Grandmother has selected potential suitors for me. They come in one by one and I'm trying to break free and run but I can't. I'm trapped. My fear of being married-off haunts my dreams for years afterwards, though it was never a real possibility. I think I was scared of was being trapped in a situation I didn't want to be in, or with a partner I didn't want to be with. Ironically years later, I learn through a series of bad ex-boyfriends that feeling isolated within a relationship – even one you thought you wanted to be in – can happen anyway.

In Indian culture you show your affection for people by feeding them. Hell, not even just affection. Someone's feeling sad? Offer them a piece of juicy mango. Child throwing a hissy fit? Offer them a chocolate bar. Someone's stopping by for tea? Offer them chicken curry with rice and naan. As a child I got very used to food being available at every turn. Something was wrong if food wasn't on offer. This way of

thinking about food used to frustrate my Mum. She came from a family where you were told, "Your eyes are bigger than your belly", or were asked "Are you *sure* you need that a second helping?", before reaching for more roast potatoes. Snacking was not allowed. Over-indulgence was frowned upon. Maybe that's what attracted here to my Dad's culture – the lack of rules, the openness and abundance. As a child, I knew which philosophy I preferred.
The way food brings people together in Indian culture is a joy. Seeing my Mum slave away by herself over a hot oven making a Sunday Roast always made me feel slightly uneasy for reasons I didn't understand. In contrast, I always enjoyed watching my Aunts and Grandmother in the kitchen, their floury hands making chapatis whilst chatting and laughing. Us children would get involved too. It didn't feel a like a chore; it felt like fun. Watching relatives cook in what can only be described as witch's cauldron in the back garden at large-scale family parties – huge pots of boiling chicken curry, various subjis, frying pakoras – whilst everyone goes about their preparations.

    Food is not mere fuel for Indians.
    Food is family.
    Food is community.
    Food is love.
    My Christmas's were unlike anyone else's I knew. They always began in a relatively normal fashion. Getting up early to open the presents

under the tree and, afterwards, tea, toast and marmalade. Over the years, Christmas became bigger and bigger as the family grew. What was a turkey dinner for five morphed into a turkey dinner for twenty-five. In order to seat that many people in my parent's modest-sized living room, all the furniture had to be removed. The boys in the family did all he heavy lifting – armchairs and coffee tables were piled up in the back garden whilst the girls, myself included, put table-cloths on trestle tables, lit candles and arranged the place settings. The dress code was always eclectic. The children and some Uncles were in Christmas jumpers with flashing Rudolph noses. My Grandmother and my Aunts in their finest saris, looking impossibly glamourous in their gleaming jewellery. There are no rules – it's Christmas our way.

Every year we attempt to put in place a seating plan, but no one sticks to it. There's always someone who wants to be close to the back door for fresh air or a quick getaway. The children want to be seated next to a parent or favourite cousin. My Grandmother needs to be sat with someone who she can converse with in Punjabi.

Christmas lunch is served buffet-style – there's enough food to feed a small army for a week. Roast turkey, roast beef, carrots, peas, parsnips, roast potatoes, Brussel sprouts, stuffing, pigs-in-blankets, cranberry sauce, mustard, three types of gravy – nothing is missed; all plates are piled high. Crackers are pulled, bad jokes told. After dinner there are eight types of dessert to choose from – coffee and tea. Once dinner is digested and the mass clear-up operation complete, it's round to my Grandmother's house next door to open presents. The children hand out the gifts and after ten minutes you can't see anyone for wrapping paper. Fatigue is setting in by this point. People have started to swap their sequins for slippers. The evening "snack" is lamb curry and naan. No cheese and biscuits here. Christmas with an Indian twist.

It amuses me when people ask whether my family and I celebrate Christmas. We celebrate it better than anyone else I know. It may not be orthodox. It's chaotic, perhaps a tad stressful at times. But it is wonderful. It's the best example of the fusion of two cultures.

In some professions you expect to see brown faces – medical, legal, I.T. My chosen career, book publishing, is still homogenously white. When I join the industry at the tender age of twenty-one, I'm struck by this fact every time I walk into the office. The diversity which I have taken for granted all my life doesn't seem to exist in my world of work. Some people ask me where I'm from. I find myself starting to tell people before they start guessing incorrectly - nine times out of ten they make assumptions that I'm Spanish or Mexican. I'm a sort of chameleon – I could be anything you want me to be.

"Where are you from?"
I'm from a land of love, hope, joy and tolerance.
I am a product of two great nations.
I am mixed-race.
I am me.

Life in Mariana
by Samuel Green

I watch the world through periscopes
underneath the sheets of black abyss
where the Angler fish dangles her bait and waits
for the bite from those who trust the stagnant
silence. My life down here remains removed
from that above. My struggling skull buckles like
the shrivelling steel of a submarine. It is
inadequate and cannot withstand brutal nature.
I struggle and survive, nomadic on these
outskirts where the thump from cityscape clubs
are mere seismic tremors. At times, I might
stumble in from grass to grate, streams to smog,
to taste his lips and her lips, the saliva and
lipstick and LSA, and hug the ivy that wraps me
in its arms, its leaves like palms, then I'll sink
back down with rocks in my pockets so deep
that I cannot tell the lighthouse from the
creatures that glow.

Party
by Neil Parker

Crazy, panic, so many people,
see through the façade of anonymous sheeple.
Must get to the food and the veggie stuff first,
grab a drink on the way to satisfy my thirst.
Didn't want to come, but felt obliged to make it,
in the end turned up, deciding to fake it.
Nod politely and mutter how are you?
truth is I don't care and neither do you.
Stand at the back and merge with the wall,
boredom too much, think I might fall.
Spy a friend trying to find peace,
go over to talk, grabbing a piece of quiche.
Sit down to complain, noise is too loud,
want to escape, flee from the crowd.
Watching people drink and playing the fool,
rather be quiet by some distant pool.
Time to go and say goodbye,
in the end I don't bother and simply fly.

by Jacqueline Chesta

The Graduate : Matthew Pierce
by Michelle Stevens

July 2008

I am Matthew Pierce, a graduate biochemist from the University of Reading. I was born and grew up in Ruislip, West London, on Saturday 13th

March 1982

I am Matthew Pierce, a homeless man who resides in a sleeping bag close by the South Ruislip tube station. I move regularly but stay close to the river Thames, running as an equator through the heart of London, where men in suits and women in baggy jeans pass by. Where midnight highway maintenance men wear high-vis gilets and young girls in pinafore dresses make their way to school.

I've walked in their shoes so many times, but how could they have ever walked in mine?

*** FIVE YEARS EARLIER ***

July 2003

Results day. You're twenty-one now and feel like you should be done with this childish anxiety, the pangs of burning in your stomach as you wait to see your future set out in a matter of numbers on a screen. University isn't like school, where you go in to collect a certificate in a sealed brown envelope, surrounded by the inquisitive, encouraging faces of the teachers who carried you through those years and physically lifted you over the final hurdles. I crawled on my own two hands and feet at University until I was practically dragging my half-dead carcass across the campus floor. *What a learning curve it will be*, they said. *The best three years of your life*, they said. I'm sitting in my living room during the longest summer holiday of my life with an endless sea of unemployment awaiting me, and a whole jar full of expectations trying to burst open like an excited puppy. My mum sits to my left watching daytime TV; my brother sits on my right eating a jam sandwich. We are my mother's children: the same children who ate jam sandwiches every day when we got in from school. The same children who painted in the garden in baggy shirts, with sticky fingers and muddy feet. And what has really changed? You expect that when you get older you suddenly get your act together and are able to get up early for meetings, to tolerate a taste for coffee and have a mind brimming with wisdom. I have three years of biochemical science: anatomy, molecular studies, human physiology, bacteriology, nutrition, genetics, cells, immunity, microbiology, brain neurology – all stacked away in that brain of mine. My brother has been through all this before me – my inspiration, a test guinea-pig, trialling life goals before I do – and as his sits with jam-coated fingers and crumbs all over his belly, I realise that we are just the same boys as we were all those years ago.

I'm clicking refresh on my computer screen, waiting for the results page to load. Two arrows are dancing in circles around each other, a tango, a dance of love, taunting me to come and play. And then the screen reloads and I'm crying, and my brother says, "Is it that bad?" And I just laugh and show them a 2:1 marked in small print next to my modules, and a sharp sense of relief floods through my veins.

July 2004

She had piercing green eyes, dark hair and freckles scattered over her nose. Eve was my everything and life quickly slotted into place. "London is the place to be" they say to all new graduates, although in hindsight we'd have been much better off dispersed across the country in affordable housing where you can actually make a living. London is a pipe dream, the big smoke, a world of infrastructure and architecture and history and men in suits alongside women in baggy jeans. Where midnight highway maintenance men wear high-vis gilets and young girls in pinafore dresses make their way to school.

It's a cold, wet evening at my parents' house when Eve suggests it. We're tucked upstairs in my bedroom which still has red and yellow wallpaper – my football team's colours. She just looks me in the eye and says it: "I could move down here," and curls her lip with a tilt of her head to brush off the question as if it's not a big deal. "London's the place to be," she says, mockingly. I reach my arm around hers and pull her close; "Alright, let's do it."

Eve adapted to my life down south with ease. She learnt that you don't have to thank the bus driver (although we've agreed that we'd like our future children to do this) and that if you say hello to people on country walks in the outskirts of London, it will be considered unusual. We don't even have a dog…how *absurd* to walk in the country! Rent stacks up with bills and electricity. We're used to this. We both did it at University, where we met back in second year. But this time it's just us with no housemates to share to costs, and the London prices are undoubtedly higher than any I'd encountered back at Uni. But it's home. And when she bounds off the tube with arms outspread, and I'm greeting her with a baked lasagne, it starts to feel like we're playing at being real adults, and we're bloody good at it!

July 2005

A high-pitched piercing noise is streaming through my ears faster than the speed of light. My lips are dry and half-open, my eyes just staring at my feet, through my feet, digging through the rug, our rug, into the foundations of our home and they just keep searching down until I can almost see the earth's core brimming and boiling into a red hot liquid. And then all is black.

"Matthew," my mum is calling me back into the room but I don't want to go back. I'm in a limbo of unconsciousness and I don't ever want to regain sanity. Insanity is my life now. Eve was my life.

It took at least an entire month for the news to sink in. On July 7th, a series of coordinated terrorist attacks devastated London. Eve was on the Piccadilly Line, on her way into work when the bomb exploded at 8:49am. We'd had our usual breakfast, Eve flitting around in the bedroom doing her make-up and trying on different jackets, struggling to agree with England's ever changeable weather. We left on time, I dropped her at the station, she smiled, said goodbye and whisked away down the alley leading to the Underground station.

"Matthew," my mother's arm over my shoulder reaches down into the core of the earth and sucks me back to reality. I look at her. Deep dark circles sag under her eyes and she is looking at my hands, my hair, and then back at my eyes again with a pleading gaze of desperation.

I am a weak man and I know that's ok as I exhale a guttural sigh followed by endless tears and I'm crying into my mother's shoulder, soddening her hair wet, boy again.

July 2006

The path to recovery never really found me, I found it. The doctor prescribed a series of antidepressants, counselling sessions, grief support groups and I even met some survivors of the London bombings who shared my devastation and despair. I spent a lot of time at Eve's grave, talking her to death as if she wasn't already, and trawling up and down the graveyards like I was deep underground with them, among the dead. I'd been signed off work for three months then went back on a part-time basis. Soon, the sick pay subsided and I was down to half pay, with a full rent and bills and life to pay for all by myself.

Eve was my girlfriend, but she was so much more than that. She was my life partner; we had locked our worlds together in a bond that we both knew was secured for life. Dogs, babies, a house with a garden and a rope swing, and maybe a tree house… we had our dreams together and that was more than some people in marriages share. But officially, she was just my girlfriend. I received no insurance following her death, no inheritance – we were both far too young to have considered wills – and neither of us had much to our names anyway. I could barely look Eve's parents in the eyes: me, the burden who dragged their child down south into London's roaring flames. And when they gave me a pitying, marbled glance through streaming tears at her funeral, I tasted bitterness, perhaps blame, culminating from somewhere in the pit of my stomach. I was a mess, hardly able to stand, a vision of a man broken from inside out. And as I sat vomiting in the crematorium toilets I contemplated how much easier it would be to end it all there and then.

No one really knew how to react to me anymore. They'd come bearing umbrellas to shelter me from the sagging grey cloud over my head and, for a brief moment, a glimpse of sunlight could be seen far in the distance, trying to break through. But when I was alone, the storm rained down and did its worst. And then one day, out of the blue, Adam introduced me to something that could ease the pain. "Just try it for a few weeks, just until you're on the mend. They all do it at work, it's harmless really," he'd said, as he snuck a stash of heroin into my satchel.

July 2007

Addiction is a funny thing. It's so f*cking good and so f*cking bad both at the same time. To watch the needle pierce my veins was so pleasurable I felt like I'd died a million times over, and then I spent the next few minutes, sometimes hours, sometimes days, dancing with the angels in heaven in my own ecstasy. Eve was there; she was always there. She looked damn good with her dark, flowing hair cascading over two huge wings which spouted from her back. She'd hop her fingers from one mole to the next across my back, smooth the stray hairs in my eyebrows and trace the outskirts of my lips with her forefinger, like she did when we were alone together. Sometimes, gently, I'd catch her laugh on a gust of wind as it twinkled through the air and illuminated the leaves on trees as it passed, like burning ember.

But when the hallucinations slipped away and I awoke from my fantasies, I'd have to relive Eve's death all over again, just like the first time.

As a biochemist, I was fascinated by the chemical reactions that were taking place in my brain. I spent my time during comedowns researching different ways, circumstances and methods to take the drug so that it could have the strongest effect. I was always craving something new, someone new. I filled an Eve-shaped hole with new girls, but unlike Eve, they had three-pronged tridents in their hands instead of wings. With them, we danced on fire whilst my life spiralled into self-destruction.

Buying heroin was a bigger financial priority than paying bills. The electricity ran out, the water stopped running, and soon the landlord – who had been so understanding at the beginning – lost patience. "I have my own family to feed;

you need to get a grip son! You need to sort this mess out, or you'll be out on the streets!" And he punched me round the face sending a blow across my jaw.

I didn't fight back. From that moment I sat in a pool of my own tears and vomit for nearly two days, as helpless as a baby. I had regressed to the neediest form of humanity, as if opening my eyes for the very first time. Every sound was new, every smell was putrid and the sour taste of the ashes of London's past played on my tongue, tarnished with pollution, corruption and… blameless. I only had myself to blame.

July 2008

I am Matthew Pierce, a graduate biochemist from the University of Reading. I was born and grew up in Ruislip, West London, on Saturday 13th

March 1982

I am Matthew Pierce, a homeless man who resides in a sleeping bag close by the South Ruislip tube station. I move regularly but stay close to the river Thames, running as an equator through the heart of London, where men in suits and women in baggy jeans pass by.

An unusually tall man is leaning against a wall, his shirt creasing as he raises his phone to his ear in what seems to be an important conversation. He is wearing a bright white shirt of a thick, expensive material, tucked into suit trousers with a smooth leather belt securing it all in place. As he leans away from the wall, he looks at his arm, dusting away any of London's filth and then he catches my eye and stumbles on his words. Almost instinctively, he looks at his watch as if to say 'Sorry, I have somewhere to be' and charges off in the opposite direction. And as I see his head bobbing above the rest of the crowd, quickly floating away in the distance, I realise that I was once him. And how, just like that, he could be me.

Here, in the background of 8 or so million people, I am at peace with the world. On these streets of London, I am finally home.

Fuchsine
by Jonathan Pizarro

Big city boys with a small-town muse wandering lanes in a hurry to succeed. That track on a loop fighting space with the fruit on your lips, Breaking mornings.

Not giving rise to much,
Printed smudge on the page before you set yourself down to wonder. And what about the walls? Save The Children. Taste the rainbow. Help the homeless. Sponsor a refugee. Have some greasy noodles, delivered to your door.

The man spread out, pushing knee onto thigh with no concept of intimacy. And tap and you're done seeking strangers in your personal illumination.

Oblivious. Often soaked all the way. Pinched between fingers and placed on the map. Departed. Returned. Rushed and eager with the promise of steam.

Tree edges. Roast beans. Bronze dogs.
Back weighing down around terracotta Victoriana semi-detached. Ages passed,
Past the concrete monsters.

More than a witness.
Centred.
Until the voyage
Out.

by Richard Wilde

The Poll Tax Demonstration
by Hilary Lynch

Faye stood outside the flat on Junction Road, the noise from passing cars behind her muffling the sound of the pounding in her ears as she stared blankly at the green, paint chipped door.

'Don't let him answer, please, don't let him answer,' she whispered to herself as she raised her clenched fist to knock.

The memory of the party at the flat earlier that month fresh in her mind, Faye stood motionless, considering whether to abort her mission and head back to the tube station. She had been too angry with Billy to get back in contact and in the weeks that had followed Faye had agonised over whether to go on the Poll Tax Demonstration at all. She knew that wild horses couldn't drag Edward to walk through the streets of London with, "a bunch of hooligans and communists," as he put it, so when Jon had called a few days before the demonstration to ask if she wanted to join him and his Militant friends on the march, Faye had been quietly delighted. Feeling a mixture of relief and trepidation, Faye made her position clear.

'I really want to go Jon, but I don't want to see Billy' said Faye, revisiting in her head Billy's hasty and guileful departure the morning after the party.

'Well there's a crowd of my commies going, and Gareth and Amber will be there too, so stick with us and just stay away from Billy. Come on Faye, we need as many people as possible to support this. Tony Benn is counting on you,' he said.

'Is he speaking at the rally?'

'And George Galloway.'

Jon proceeded to entice Faye with the list of celebrity speakers, and it didn't take much more persuasion for Faye to agree to meet them at the flat on the morning of the demonstration.

'You won't even know Billy's there,' Jon reassured.

And with that promise in mind, Faye had taken the tube across London that morning, arriving outside the flat before eleven o'clock. Closing her eyes, she took a deep breath and knocked nervously on the door. The sound of movement within made Faye's heart thump faster, each beat in time to the sound of heavy footsteps down the staircase. As the door opened, she quietly let out a sigh of relief at the sight of Jon standing in the doorway.

'Billy said he heard someone knock. Come on in Faye,' he said opening the door wide. 'We're just about ready. Go straight up to the kitchen, I'll only be a few minutes.'

Sitting alone on the grubby sofa, Faye anxiety about the day rose again, this time from the pit of her stomach. Spotting a half-drunk bottle of Tequila on the kitchen worktop, she toyed with the idea of downing a mouthful, but before she had time to get her hands on the beckoning elixir it was too late. Dressed in a black Sex Pistols t-shirt and ripped jeans, Billy slunk into the kitchen with hands wedged deep in his pockets, his eyes darting to meet hers.

'Hi Faye…. long-time no see. How are you?' he uttered cautiously.

'Fine,' she answered curtly, before turning her attention to the cigarette burns that adorned the arm of the sofa.

Gareth's dulcet tones rose up from the landing to the kitchen, breaking the awkward silence.

'Billy, Faye, we're going now!'

Arriving at Tufnell Park station, Gareth, Jon, Amber, Billy and Faye caught the tube to Elephant and Castle, then walked to the gates of Kennington Park and on to the demonstration meeting place where they met up with Jon's Militant comrades. Faye kept her distance from Billy throughout the journey, and inside the park Faye latched on to Jon as they strolled towards the assembly point.

It was a beautiful spring day with hordes of people gathering in good spirits, giving rise to a carnival atmosphere in the air. Musical bands and jugglers entertained the crowds as whole families, mothers, fathers, grandparents, young children and babies in pushchairs, stood side by side along with working adults and students to protest the unfairness of the Poll Tax Bill. A real buzz could be felt vibrating through the crowd who were there to make their voices heard, feeling that collectively they could make a difference, that they could change not only the policy, but perhaps even the government.

At one thirty in the afternoon, the crowd started to move forward through the gates of Kennington Park. Billy and Amber walked behind Gareth, Jon and Faye, all holding their banners, declaring 'No to Poll Tax' and 'Can't Pay, Won't Pay,' high in the air, chanting in time with the stewards with loud-hailers, as they moved towards the rally which was to be held in Trafalgar Square.

Following the crowd up Kennington Road to Westminster Bridge, Faye moved between Jon and Gareth, trying to avoid contact with Billy, while he and Amber chatted behind. When they reached bridge over the River Thames, Faye looked out across the water to the Houses of Parliament, Saint Paul's Cathedral and Westminster Abbey in the distance. The river sparkled in the sunlight, and Faye decided she was glad that she had come after all, to witness this perfect united front against the Thatcher government.

Across Westminster Bridge, they entered Parliament Square, then taking a right turn on Whitehall they made their way towards to Nelsons Column.

It wasn't until they got to Downing Street that Faye noticed that the atmosphere had changed somewhat, and she watched as police poured into Whitehall causing a nervousness to ripple through the crowd. Suddenly the march ground to a halt and Gareth pointed out the mounted police at the far end of the street.

Word of mouth spread quickly through the crowd that Trafalgar Square had reached full capacity and realising there was no more room for anyone in Whitehall, the disgruntled crowd began to call out in anger. Unable to move forward or backwards because of the stationary crowd and the mounted police either end, Faye felt like a caged animal. She looked on at the police who stood menacingly side by side to form an insurmountable barrier on either side of the street. Beyond the police line Faye could see a group of skinheads filing up a side street which led onto Whitehall, directly opposite where she and the others were standing. Realising their presence would cause trouble, Faye looked around for an escape route, but there was nowhere to go. Billy sidled up towards Faye.

'This doesn't look good Faye,' he said, scanning the unfolding scene before them.

'Well you're pretty good at sneaking off without anyone noticing, perhaps you could find us a way out,' she scoffed back at him.
He let out a heavy sigh.

'Okay, I get it, you're angry with me and that's why you haven't returned my calls or been in town recently. Can we just move on?'

An image of Billy and Heather together popped into Faye head, but she chose to use Edward as her excuse for not being in contact; she wanted to steer clear of the 'why was your ear suckered to spare room door?' conversation. 'I haven't been in town because Edward and I have been busy looking at houses. His mother's giving us the deposit on a place in Richmond. And besides I've no reason to come into central London anymore,' she said nonchalantly.
Faye felt a rush of adrenaline at the thought of punishing him, and she tried desperately not to smirk.

'Where is Tory Boy today then? Hanging out with those other five escaped Nazi war criminals hiding in Britain?' Billy snapped.

A group of skinheads had wrapped black scarves around their faces and were trying to break though the police lines. Feeling anxiety rise within the crowd, mixed with the sarcasm and tension in Billy's voice, Faye turned to him full of rage.

'What is it with you and Edward, what do you have against him?' she shouted

'What do I have against him?! It's people like him, voting this government into power, that are to blame for the state of this country. People like Edward who work for huge corporations, trampling over the workers, making the division between the haves and have not's even greater,' he shouted over the rising din.

'Hang on a minute, he's only just landed his first proper job and you're blaming him for Thatcher's policies!' she shouted, remembering the words that Edward had used to shut her down. Gareth, Jon and Amber standing to one side of Billy looked on apprehensively.

'Listen you two, stop arguing, this is bad. We can't get out of here,' said Gareth, flinching as a stone aimed at the police line flew into the crowd. Police began to grab at the marauding skinheads who were trying to break through the line of officers.

'Go on then, tell us which bank he's working for?' said Billy, as people around them began to shuffle backwards.

Faye hesitated, knowing exactly how he would react.

'Barclays,' she said quietly, hoping the rising noise of the crowd would drown her out, 'not that it's any of your business.'

'Barclays!' he yelled.

'Is it just me or is there an echo out here!' Faye cried out, looking past Billy to the others.

'I might have known! Don't you mean Boerclays?! He's working for a bank that supports the South African government, a bank that supports apartheid?!'

'It's a job, and he can't turn it down based on your politics. And anyway, Barclays pulled out of South Africa a few years ago, and Nelson

Mandela was freed in February this year, you know that,' said Faye, feeling ashamed of herself.

'Only because of people like you and I, who went on anti-apartheid demonstrations, went to the Nelson Mandela Tribute concerts, boycotted Barclays and brought down the share price! We made them pull out, we made the difference, or have you forgotten all of that? And Barclays are still funding Mugabe in Zimbabwe; what about all the human rights abuses there? As for Edward working for them, it's immoral,' he said turning his head from Faye in disgust.

As the skinheads punched, kicked and spat at the police officers, the crowd began to jostle nervously, and Faye was pushed flat up against Billy. She stared up at him in fury.
'That's immoral?! At least he has some dignity, he doesn't go around drugging vulnerable women, sleeping with them and then sneaking off the next morning! He's a decent, hardworking man and he doesn't expect something for nothing!'

'Well it's nice to know you have such a high opinion of me! You make me out to sound like a rapist!'

'Well, if the hat fits! Why Billy? Why?! She's my sister and I told you that she was ill, and you took advantage of her! I said, 'please keep Gareth away, you know how he letches' not '*please,* feel free to supply her with drugs and then sleep with her!' Faye shouted.

'*Hey*…..what's that supposed to mean,' said Gareth slighted.

'Sorry Gareth, but come on, when you're drunk….'

Billy sighed.

'Look, I *was* making sure Gareth didn't start leering again…'

'For fuck sak…. I'm still here!' cried Gareth.

'…. but that meant that I spent time with her, and she asked for the drugs, and you know that I'm a generous guy and, okay, maybe I should have stopped it sooner, …. but I was so off my face that night. That sister of yours can't half drink; I didn't know what I was doing.'

'And there it is! There's always an excuse, isn't there Billy!' Faye spat vociferously at him. 'It's never your fault, is it?! She suffers from depression Billy!'

'I thought it would cheer her up and she was *very* persuasive!'

'Stop!!' Faye bellowed, gasping in revulsion. '*You* are so disgusting! Just get away from me, I hate you!' Faye screamed up at Billy, as she tried unsuccessfully to push herself back from him.

'Hey, I think there's something going on further back towards Parliament Square,' said Jon, looking anxiously over the top of heads, the sound of breaking glass intensifying.

'Oh, don't get on your high horse with me Faye Ryan! You grew up on that council estate and now you've abandoned your principles to be with Edward, the banker, with his wealthy parents in Surrey. How can you stand there and pretend to be part of this, when really all you are is a hypocrite and a traitor to your roots?! Go on, go home to Edward; shouldn't you be in your new kitchen cooking a meal for Tory Boy and his Managing Director! You make me sick, you don't belong here anymore!'

A handful of skinheads had broken through the police lines and were running up and down the street, as a man came pushing through the crowds of protestors shouting 'We need to get the kids out of here now'.
Faye eyes fixed onto Billy's and she felt her throat tighten and a lump rise to the surface.

'I belong here more than you……' she began through gritted teeth, '…. you arrogant, middle class, champagne socialist! You wave a placard here, pretending you know what it was like for people like me growing up. Well I've got news for you, you don't know, you have no idea. You never had to watch the pride disappear from your father's face when the bailiffs took *everything* we had; you never had to hear the chants every day at school because of the raggedy clothes you wore; you never lay awake in bed unable to sleep because you were so cold and hungry, sore from the bruises and….' She hesitated. 'I've had to do things I'm not exactly proud of to claw my way out of poverty. It's my family who are the people you say you're fighting for today, so don't tell me I don't belong

here; it's not me who's pretending to be part of this, it's you,' and she pushed her 'Can't Pay; Won't Pay' board into Billy's chest, and forced her way through the crowd back towards the Parliament Square end of Whitehall.
Wiping the tears from her face she pushed through the army of protestors, the noise of the crowd changing from a cry to a roar, then a few seconds later Billy's voice rang out in the distance behind her.

'Faye…stop. Wait.'

Moving swiftly, Faye made her way forward, the crowd thinning as got closer to Whitehall entrance. Bottles smashed on the ground in front of her and stones whizzing above her head as she watched in horror a gang of masked skinheads run ahead of her holding missiles in their hands. The shouting escalating, Faye instinctively stopped dead in her tracks and waited, then all at once the crowd turned towards her, running in the opposite direction as they pushed past her screaming.

As the fog of protestors starting to clear, Faye caught sight of the mounted police charging into the crowd with batons. Frozen in terror, Faye watched on as a black horse galloped forward, the policeman on top with baton raised and visor down, coming straight at her. Closing her eyes and bracing herself for the impending pain she was about to feel, Faye suddenly felt a force throw her to one side and she fell onto the ground. Opening her eyes, Faye looked up to see the baton fall hard on the back of Billy's head, before he slumped down onto his knees, then fell forward, blood spilling out into his hair and down onto his t-shirt. Faye scrambled over to Billy as he lay motionless on the ground. Taking his head in her hands, she tried desperately to stop the bleeding.

'Billy wake up, please wake up….,' she screamed.

Rushing towards a female officer at the end Whitehall, Faye pleaded desperately.

'Please, my friend is hurt, he needs an ambulance.'

Taking one look at her bloodstained hands and clothes the police officer spoke into her walkie-talkie for a few seconds, then turned towards Faye.

'An ambulance will be here soon, wait with him,' she commanded, the lack of real concern etched on her hardened face.

The ride to hospital was slow, despite the siren and the blue light, as the ambulance meandered its way through great swaths of people and swarms of traffic. Reaching the accident and emergency entrance, Billy was wheeled on a trolley out of the ambulance and into the hospital, while Faye was told to sit in the waiting area.

Several hours passed before Faye was allowed onto the ward. Walking to the far end where Billy lay on a bed, his head in bandages and his arm strapped to a blood pressure machine, Faye quietly approached him.

'How are you?' she whispered when he finally opened his eyes.

'Head hurts a lot, but I'm ok,' said Billy.

'Don't ever do that to me again,' she scolded gently.

'What?'

'Jump in front of me and get yourself nearly killed.'

'I don't know what you mean. I just gave you a bit of a shove for implying I was a rapist!' he smiled.

'You really scared the bejesus out of me, you moron,' she smirked.

He looked across at her and frowned.

'Look Faye, while we're on the subject of morons, I am really sorry for what happened. But I don't want us to fall out over this…… I miss you, I miss talking to you about things. I even miss you talking about Tory Boy.'

Faye smiled across at him.

'I've kind of missed talking to you too, but Heather's not well.'

Billy reached across and gently took hold of her fingers.

'Are we still friends?' he asked coyly.

Faye's heart sank as she stared back at him, suicide threats ringing in her ears through the dawning realisation that friendship was furthermost from her mind.

Images of Eastbourne
by Angela Narayn

Jangled notes through a seagull sky,
his skin leathered,
lean with wanderings.
A cap upturned, hopeful, on curled edged cover:
a dog lies, ragged ear,
half-cocked, and drooping eye, watching.

Hesitating,
fumbling for change amid plaintive vocals:
'All along the watchtower.'
Swimming along pensioner filled benches,
and fish and chips lunches
in polystyrene boxes.
Through wheelchairs and mobility scooters,
and foreign students, like clouds,
drifting.

Babies pass in buggies,
drunk on sea air,
sun creamed children
with lolly red lips,
and bucket and spades trailing,
and trainers flashing.
Roller skaters, free-styling,
and a strange army
with dreadlocks and drumbeats,
tattooed and pierced,
strutting their wares.
Ahead,

stripy deckchairs and bandstand protruding,
and the wind washed pier, an arthritic limb,
reclining.

The polished pebbled beach and the sea brave,
with seaweed toes and salt dipped tongues,
heads bobbing like toffee apples.
Limbs askew
angled through waves,
slimy and slick like the back of toads.
And the seabed dark,
crab clawed and eel soft,
beady-eyed and jellyfish stinging.

The sharpness of coin, tossed one on another;
he doesn't look up as bodies move past.
In the night,
upturned,
facing the cracks in the ceiling,
life clings like a shadow.
His downward glance,
lank hair falling,
folded over his guitar like an attentive lover.

His notes linger,
over eggshell flesh,
and barrel chest, crackling,
a thread of saliva falling.
Midst slanting waves and crooked shoreline,
halcyon days of youth return,
silver and gold, flashing.

Fierce and fearless,
free jumping, over walls and railings,
wavelike.
Over ornamental flower beds
and fairy lit pathways,
past rough sleepers in dark corners.
Across driftwood,
flint and sharp shell beach,
shifting.
Under aching stars,
the belly of sea
hissing and heaving,
beating out its ceaseless rhythm.
Sucking me in,
Jonah like,
deep inside its glittering belly.
Amoebic,
returning to the mud and slime
of shapeless form and impenetrable darkness.

by Hannah Gravestock

The Thing About Geoff
by Chris Miller

'Yeah, just pull in here, past that silver one there's a bit more space… and the plot's just opposite.'

He caught sight of it in the rear-view mirror for the first time -- a mass of green, everything as high as the knee and higher in places. 'It's pretty wild.'

'Yes… the poor guy wasn't well -- 'depressed', Dawn said; he's not been for six months apparently. Nobody's heard from him, it's really sad.'

'Which one's Dawn?'
She spoke over him excitedly: 'come and have a look at the view out the back, you can see the castle!'

As the shutting of the car door broke the tranquillity, a head popped up – they'd not even seen him when they pulled in. An inquisitive, wide-eyed glance from between a neatly shaved line of white beard and moustache and two wispy, white brows up top.

'Hello there, are you the new plot owners?', asked the squatting gentleman – and he truly looked the gentleman, head to toe in tweed.

'We are! James,' he offered a hand – 'and this is Olivia. Nice to meet you. Which one's yours?'

'I've got 62'.

James didn't receive a hand back because, firstly, the man hadn't noticed, and secondly, both of his hands were busy. One was outstretched and open with a scruffy robin shuttling forward, taking pieces of still-writhing maggot from it, retreating, before repeating the routine. The other was dipping into a tackle box ready to replenish the supply.

'Took a while to get him to do this! Or her, I've never been sure. I'm Geoff, pleased to meet you.'

*

'Your corn's looking good, Geoff'. James wanted any excuse to talk to him.

'Yes, I'm rather pleased with it, it's been a good year for the sweetcorn, all this sun – I should be able to start harvesting the rest next week. I've had nine ears so far and I've counted 35 to come. Just hope the rats don't get it before I do.' He was using a pocket knife to cut the cob from the plant, peeling back the leaves from around the edge, and then expertly slicing away the top and tail, leaving a perfect, gold, kernel-laden ear.

'Rats?!'

'Little devils come off the fields, sniff it out and are up there… ha, I was going to say 'like a rat up a drainpipe'!' Geoff chuckled and James joined him, such was Geoff's infectious nature. James absent-mindedly stared at Geoff, thinking *he could tell a story about painting a wall and you'd want to gather everyone round to listen.*

'Your corn's a bit behind mine, of course, as it went in later, but it's in good nick, James, you've done really well.'

'Not bad for a first attempt, we're pretty happy with it.

'I'll bet, you've really turned this plot round.'

A compliment like that from Geoff was like winning the lottery.

'I'll let you get on, give me a shout if you need anything, and help yourself to my rake if you need it.'

*

Olivia was staring out the back of the plot, her expression one of ease, contentment.

'God! You scared me!' James had put his arms around her waist; she'd zoned out from the allotment and was lost in her view.

'Sorry, I thought you'd have heard me coming.' He had his top off, was glistening with sweat and was puffing from hacking at the deep root of a bramble.

'Look at him Liv.' She turned to her right, towards plot 62. Geoff was picking his jostaberries ('they're like a cross between a gooseberry and a blackcurrant', he'd said, handing James one to try) and putting them into a tub that used to be home to 500 grams of margarine.

'He's just so great. You know, he told me earlier that he fishes too – caught a 25 pound pike last week. The thing about Geoff is he knows something about *everything*. His brain is like an encyclopaedia.'

'James, I sometimes wonder if you like Geoff more than me.'

'I do!' He smirked. 'Maybe I'll see if he wants to come to the cinema tonight instead, you hate the cinema anyway.' He skipped off back down the allotment to the fork which was stood upright, tines several inches into the earth, half-removed bramble root by its side.

*

'Do you eat blackberries?'

'Yes, we love them'.
Geoff handed over a bagful. 'They make lovely jam if you're interested. Or crumble.'

'Oh thanks, Geoff, that's really good of you.'

'No problem, and help yourself to more if ever I'm not here, I've got more than I can manage by myself.'

'Do you live by yourself, Geoff?'

'Me? Oh yes, always have, it suits me well. I'm very particular.'

'You never married then? Sorry, tell me if I'm prying.'

'No, no that's fine, I don't mind. I just never met the right woman. I courted a few and it never went any further than that. I don't worry too much about it, I've had a good life. Kept myself occupied.'

James smiled and Geoff put his thick, tweet-covered arm around his shoulder.

'When are you two having children then?'

*

As Olivia pulled up next to Geoff's car, she felt uneasy, as if she were being watched. Because she was. Geoff was just the other side of his runner beans, she saw him as she headed towards her shed.

'Morning Geoff.'

He was with someone -- a skinny, spiky looking character with a sharp nose and grey skin. He didn't smile at her.

'Hello there, Olivia. Have you met Michael? He has 61, the other side of me. Grows terrific beetroot, you should see the size of it.'

Michael nodded but didn't break into a smile. Olivia said hello, shook a limp hand and went to get on with her odd jobs – a bit of watering, a bit of weeding. She had a fire going in the corner of the plot as she worked as they had uncovered a fair amount of wood along the way -- they could not work out what the previous owner used it for, but there were offcuts everywhere.

'He didn't half use a lot of wood'. Geoff was leaning on one of his plot marker posts. 'God knows what he was thinking, poor bloke.'

'What was he called, Geoff?'

'Patrick his name was. He got a dog, I think, that's why he stopped coming. Could only cope with one thing at once. I always liked him.'

*

'He won't mind, honest – he said we can help ourselves to stuff.'

'That was the rake! He didn't say we could poke about on the rest of his plot!'

'Oh don't be silly, he loves us! He'd like to know we're taking an interest. Besides, it's a public footpath!'

'*That* bit is' -- she pointed to the footpath that ran between each plot.

James hopped over Geoff's higgledy-piggledy fence, made from old shower screens and greenhouse panels. It was a matter of seconds before he was out of her view, such was the success of Geoff's blackberries this year -- masses of thick, fulsome bushes which were as tall as she was. The tomatoes to their left were clustered to the point where they too formed a barrier.

'Liv.' James wasn't shouting but he was making himself heard.

'What? I'm not coming, it feels wrong.'

'Liv! LIV!' Now he was shouting.
She panicked and jumped the panels, zipped between the tomatoes following the path that James had and she could see him the other side of a row of thick-stemmed, dying sunflowers.

He was staring down at a patch of earth which was partially-covered by black fabric liner and partially-covered by one of the Dalek-shaped compost heaps at the back of the plot. As she got closer she saw that James was stood over a clenched fist. A very pale, decaying clenched fist, protruding from the ground.

'Why are you back here?' They'd not heard Geoff's car pull in.

by Thomas Ryan

Big Boys Cry Too
by Jordan Friend

You cried when you realised, not happy or sad just relieved.
You're…. Gay.
Getting it out in the open was so liberating…
Like bursting out of a glass coffin shattering your own perceptions
you are free to be 'me',
You feel brand new,
moulded separate from yourself with tears streaming furrows into your skin,
soaking off the lies and misconceptions you always held about yourself,
You're… Gay.
The word enraptures you, captures you
, and you are grateful for it, wrapping it around yourself, Gay,
Gay,
Gay as in happy,
Gay as in liking Men and…
others.

You wanted to kill yourself for so long
but you are past that now
You are past the times of wanting to drag that rusty nail from the shed
Into your
Veins.
And forget---Everything.

Gay is the best catchall because you know that
you are definitely not *Straight*,
and opening this up now you are no longer sure
of anything,
you have rejected the binary,
male or female,
straight or gay,
You are *Discovering Yourself* again.
Nothing is clean cut anymore
your identity is being rewritten,
the one and zeros of you are different now.
You are a new machine rewired
relearning you are infant again,
touch starved and impatient you are
Learning.

You have disassembled the matrix and are
making yourself new.
Like lightning striking honey you are bursting
onto the scene all energy and sweetness and
severity
You are a boy made of magic and you are finding
it organically.

You are ready for the chills for the thrills of a
new you,
you are Excited for it and you are ready for
Loveeeeeee.

An all-encompassing *Fuck You* Love.
One to yell from the rooftops,
about someone special,
organic,
orgasmic
Loveeeeee.
You are Fireworks exploding in the daytime,
unexpected but no less irreverent,

a shout from the rooftops
I AM NEW!

And even though you have been crying,
you remember that Big Boys Cry Too
you are just *You*
spreading open your curtains in the search of all
things bold and
NEW.

No Offence
by Andy Lewis

When did you know you were gay? How did you know you were gay? When did you come out? That's so late, why did you take so long? That's so young, how were you sure? Are your parents ok with it? Are you sad that you'll never have children? Do you think you will ever get married? I want to go to a gay wedding. I could tell you were gay, no offence. *I'm* ok with it; *I* don't have a problem with it. It's kind of obvious though. No offence. What do you do in bed? Are you the guy or the girl? Are you the train or the tunnel? What does 'top' and 'bottom' mean? Do you let guys fuck you? That must hurt. Isn't that kind of dirty? I would never do anything there. That place is exit only. Do you have grindr? That's so funny. Don't all gay guys sleep around? Do you have a *partner*? So are you the girl in the relationship? You think like a girl though, right? All your friends are girls, right? Can you help me with this girl? What about me… are you attracted to me? You have thought about it, right? You are… that's weird, no offence. I'm not gay. You're not attracted to me…why not? Do you like *manly* guys or *gay* guys? Do you like straight guys? Why do all gay guys like straight guys? Have you ever been with a girl? Have you seen Brokeback Mountain? Have you seen Modern Family? Do you watch Will and Grace? You should, you would like it. I know a gay guy. I'll set you up. Do you know each other? You would be so cute together. Gay men are so cute. Gay men are so fun. I like gay men, but I don't like lesbians. I'm ok with gay people, but I don't understand bisexuals. I don't mind people being gay, but not like *gay* gay. Let's go on a girl's day out. You're just one of the girls, you know? Are you good with makeup? No? You're such a bad gay. Why do gay guys wear makeup? It looks so tacky, no offence. Why do gay men all talk like that? Gay pride looks so fun! I don't understand gay pride. Why isn't there a straight pride? Gay marriage is legalised now, so what's the point in gay pride? Gays have equal rights now. No one cares if you're gay. Homophobia is bad, but it works both ways. Homophobic people are just secretly gay. Do you like my outfit? You're like, totally my gay best friend. Let me introduce you, this is my *gay friend*…What should I wear? Can we go shopping? I thought gay guys had good style, no offence. Do you like Lady Gaga? Do you like Tom Daley? Do you like Elton John? How do you know if someone's gay? I have such a good gaydar. What about that guy, do you think he's gay? He doesn't *look* gay. He doesn't *seem* gay. He seems normal to me. Ugh, that's so gay. No, I don't mean it like that. I mean it like stupid. What do you mean I shouldn't say that? What do you mean that's offensive? You can't say anything anymore. Don't get offended so easily. Don't be so sensitive. Don't be so dramatic. Gay people are so dramatic. I can say that, I have a gay friend. You don't mind, right? I'm not homophobic, I love gay people. Gay people are so funny. We should go to a gay club. That would be so funny. Men are so awful, except you because you're gay. Women are hard work, gay guys have it so easy. I wish I was gay. I'm not gay though. I'm not gay. I don't mind gay people, but…

The Office Treehouse
by Vivienne Burgess

A small office space. Desk, shelf and chair. All fixed to the wall and supported by a sliding platform, assembled under a bridge in Valencia, Spain. None of the locals know it's there.
The designer enjoys his floating office in private, revelling at the achievement with his feet up on the desk, a secret sniggering, tucked like a wasp's nest in the underpass.

Soon the feeling fades. The designer becomes fidgety, losing track of his sketches. He watches a stack of tracing papers slip and flit like feathers onto the road below. He decides to hire an intern to help with actualising his grand designs.

The interviews take place at the floating office. He instructs the interviewees to ring the brass bell pull upon first arriving, and then he cranks the platform across the short length of the bridge, making use of the existing beams as wheel tracks, to the other side, where the upward sloping land allows him to step on and off the platform. He calls this the reception area.

During the first interview, the young hopeful sits while the designer stands, his desk between them. There is only one chair. The designer asks the young man, 'So what inspires you?' The young man coughs. He pulls on the cuff of his ironed shirt. 'Ergonomic structures,' he says. The designer makes a note in his pad. The young man, striking confidence, offers the question back to him. The designer looks up. 'What inspires *me*? Blanket forts,' he says.

The second interview goes better. Once again, at the ringing of the brass bell pull, the designer cranks the platform across to the reception area. 'This is incredible,' says the young man awaiting him. This interviewee is dressed casually in plain, comfortable clothes. The designer dresses this way too. They shake hands. 'May I?' asks the young man. The designer ticks off another box in his head. The young man steps aboard and the designer starts cranking. 'Really, this is amazing,' he says with a hand outstretched, touching the wall as they move. 'Thank you,' says the designer. 'It took a long time.'

*

A week passes without further visit. The designer is at his desk on the platform when the brass bell goes. He looks across to the reception area and sees the chain for the bell swinging gently, but no person to have pulled it. He stands slowly and cranks the platform across, imagining, remembering, something he'd read recently about a family, terrorized, a bear having found its way into their home.

The platform connects with the wall and shudders. The designer clamps on the wheel brake. He calls out to whoever is there but no one responds. Then a child pokes his head out sideways from behind a pillar supporting the road up to the bridge.

'Hello there,' says the designer. 'Hello,' says the boy. 'Are you lost?' 'No.' 'Where are your parents?' 'At home.' The boy does not move from behind the pillar. The designer is at a loss. 'Are you the designer man?' asks the boy. 'Is this is the office treehouse?'

The designer laughs. 'It is. I am.' The boy still does not move. 'Would you like to see?' The boy nods. 'You'll have to come closer,' says the designer. A moment's hesitation and the boy steps forward.

The designer gives, by nature, a quick tour of the office space. 'Take a seat,' he says. 'Wouldn't want you to fall.' The boy sits, glancing furtively from the objects close around him to the designer's face, as if checking for permission. 'How did you know I was here?' asks the designer. The boy fixes his gaze on the papers spread atop the desk. 'My brother came here.' 'Oh, what's his name?' says the designer. 'I must have interviewed him.' 'Sebastian,' says the boy. The designer smiles.

He learns the boy is eight years old and his name is Diego. Diego is not at school right now because the school is closed for the holidays. Sebastian is one of four older siblings. 'Nicolás, Sebastian, Valeria and Sofía,' says Diego. 'Sofía is a brain doctor.'

'Very smart,' says the designer. He does not have any juice to give the boy, only the carton of

UHT milk he uses for his coffee. 'What about Valeria?' he asks. 'What does she do?'

'Valeria is at the university. She's going to be a doctor as well.' Diego sips the milk from a cardboard takeaway cup. 'Nicolás fell of his motorbike. He's stays in bed all day.'

The designer coughs, feeling fear again, the fear of the intruder bear. In child-like steamroller fashion, Diego continues.

'Sebastian was working in the kitchen at a restaurant, but they made him leave.'

'Yes, he must be in need of work,' says the designer, glad to have the topic changed. 'I'd like to hire him. Would you tell him that? I've been trying to call.'

Diego sips the milk. 'Sebastian is having a baby with Luciá, who's his girlfriend. But they don't love each other very much.'

Diego slurps the last of his milk and holds out the empty cup for the designer to take. He does. He puts it high on the shelf. Diego watches the traffic moving slowly below.

'No,' he says again. 'They don't love each other very much.'

'I'm sure they'll love the baby when it comes along.'

Diego shrugs. 'I'm hungry.'

'Alright,' says the designer. 'I don't have any food. Let's get you back.'

'Okay,' says Diego.

'It was nice meeting you. Could you ask your brother to call me? Just tell him, call Fernando, if he still wants the job.'

'Okay,' says Diego, and the designer cranks them back to the other side.

*

Weeks pass before Diego's next visit. The designer is in a good mood. He has been putting things on paper. This time, after the bell rings, and the designer cranks the platform across, Diego is not hiding behind a pillar. The designer thinks he sees a smile.

'Diego! How are you?' he says. Diego steps onto the platform without looking at him.

'I want to see the treehouse again, please.'

'Alright,' says the designer.

Back in the office space, Diego sits at the desk once more and the designer goes through the rough plans for his next big venture. Diego touches the paper with his fingertips, ever so gently.

'Careful,' the designer touches Diego's hand. 'Don't smudge.'

'How long does it take to make?' Diego asks.

'I don't know,' says the designer. 'I have yet to make it.'

Straightening his back, the designer knocks the shelf, and a forgotten cardboard cup falls from the top into the noise of traffic below. Only the designer sees this. Diego doesn't notice.

'I'd need some help with it actually,' says the designer. 'You know, your brother never called.'

Diego spreads his hands flat on the desk. He looks up.

'Can I live here?'

The designer splutters, laughing. He gathers quickly, from Diego's face, that this was an erroneous response.

'No,' he says, composed. 'I'm afraid you can't. Your parents would miss you too much.'

'No they wouldn't,' Diego muttered. His gaze wandering again off the edge of the platform.

'They wouldn't like you staying with a stranger,' says the designer.

'You're only a stranger to them,' Diego says, ready for such an argument.

'You know, that's very true,' says the designer. 'But still. It's just not possible right now.'

'When then?'

There are tears in the boy's eyes. He has not yet been taught to hide them. Suddenly the designer feels sick at the absurdity of their situation. He thinks he should probably reach to comfort the boy. He folds his arms instead.

'I'm sorry, Diego. We cannot be friends.'

The boy digests this. Then he stands.

'Crank me back. I want to go home.'

'Alright. Would you like to help me? It's quite heavy.'

The boy sniffs and wipes his cheeks. 'Okay.'

Together they crank the platform back to the other side.

*

Not twenty-four hours pass before the designer is interrupted yet again by the brass bell ringing in his reception area. He looks sternly at the bank. The culprit is blocked once more by a supporting pillar. The designer ignores them, leans back over his papers, but whoever it is yanks on the bell a second time.

The designer completes his final crank under the bridge with excessive force and the platform ricochets against the wall with a bang. A young woman stands before him on the bank, visibly alarmed at this loud arrival. The designer remains on the platform, hand on the crank, held still by her immediate beauty. Her outfit is in no way revealing, but he has no trouble imagining what's beneath. The designer straightens his back, conscious of the creative state his hair must be in.

'Hello,' he says. 'Can I help you?'

She looks him up and down, firm footed, unimpressed.

'Are you the one in charge?'

'I— yes, I suppose. It's only me here.'

Her face is unchanged. 'So you know my brother then,' she says.

The designer brightens. 'Sebastian? Yes—'

'Diego.' She glares. 'I know he's visited you a few times.'

The designer stiffens. 'Yes, but I didn't invite him.' He can see disgust in her features, a ferocious outrage expertly contained. He doesn't know what to say first. 'Your brother, Sebastian, I interviewed him some weeks ago—he must have told Diego where—'

'He is not to come here again,' she says. 'You are to leave him alone.'

'Yes— my god, of course! I would never... I don't intend—I hope you don't think... Nothing has happened. We just... drank milk.'

He thinks he sees a twitch in the woman's mouth, as if she might laugh.

'I don't care what you drank,' she says. 'You are not to see Diego again. If he comes here, you are to turn him away. Do not touch him. Do not talk to him.'

The designer laughs desperately, stepping off the platform to approach her.

'Please, there's been a misunderstanding... I never caught your name?'

'Valeria Pérez.'

The designer opens his mouth to respond in kind, but Valeria Pérez is faster.

'I don't want to know your name, sir. If you tell me, I'll report it to the police. I don't want to do that.'

'Well, no, because there's really no need.' The designer smiles broadly, sweating, holding his hands together. 'Please, Miss Pérez. I'm no threat to Diego. I have no issue with never seeing him again. If I may, Valeria... I know a little of what's happening at home.'

She flinches from him, mouth twisted with loathing.

'You know nothing of our family! Who do you think you are? You are no one! You go build another tiny house under some other bridge, and you stay away from us!'

Valeria Pérez is shaking. She stares the designer down. He's torn at first; he wants to compliment her eyes, so wet and fierce, so brown and pretty, but her mouth is the hardest line he's ever seen, so he retreats, tripping to step backwards onto the platform. She smooths her hair back. She lets her breath go. There are nail marks in her upper arms. She spits and points down on the bank where it lands.

'You *stay. Away.*'

The traffic moves slowly past the foot of the sloping bank. He doesn't know which way she went. In his head she walked right into the road and the traffic parted to let her through.
He cranks the platform back across the length of the bridge and sits down at his desk. He is shaking too, just like Valeria. This ties them together, he thinks. They are both upset. Perhaps he should try calling Sebastian to set things straight, to offer him the job once more, to ask about Luciá and the baby… But there'd be no answer. The designer knows this. To this family he is a monster, and knowing this feels more deadly than falling.

The designer collects his papers into one pile. He was almost excited about this one. Now he is disgusted with himself. This is the boy's fault. He should have pushed Diego down the hill the first time he showed up at the reception area. The designer feels like shouting, having his side heard by anyone within earshot. He grips his desk. He tries yanking it from the wall but his fixtures are too strong. He at swipes his pencil case and it falls off the platform, unzipped, spewing its contents of precise and delicate instruments into the air.

Valeria Pérez is the perverted one. The whole rotten Pérez family. They've done this. The office is not a dungeon. It's not a trap. It's just a platform, for God's sake. It's just a blanket fort! And they've ruined it. They've outright ruined it. It's ruined. He should just kill himself. That's what they want.

The designer resolves to follow Miss Pérez's instruction. He will dismantle the floating platform. He will go somewhere new, somewhere entirely unheard of, he'll detach from society. He'll build another spectacle, another breath-taking homage to the faded spirit of his childhood, and he'll keep it to himself. Keep it hidden. The way it has to be, apparently, when your turn is over.

by Thomas Ryan

Fear of Love
by Eden Kofi Joseph

How many seconds have I been able to look my father in both eyes for?

One?

Two?

Three?

Let me tell you a secret…

I have flashbacks

My godfather in his garden in Ruislip

His huge feet planted over the weed-ridden patio

Bending at the knees

Launching his daughter into the air

Her voice bellowing from her tiny lungs with laughter

And joy…

In the photo that captured that moment

You could see their eyes were locked to each other's

The longest I have stared into another mans eyes?

Probably the minute before a madness was about to kick off

Or that three or four seconds sitting in the barber's chair…

Reverse mirror in his hand

Eyebrows raised expectantly

Like a boy handing his end of year grades to his Dad

A nod

Moments of expectation

Of build up…

All for a nod

"Ye, that's calm man"

How many seconds have you been able to look your friend in the eye for?

Evenin' premier league catch ups on the Uxbridge road

Sam's chicken spicy 2 for 2 and glucose fizzy strawberry Mirinda

Or one or two beers in the least racist looking pub we could find

I wonder if talk of women, boxing and football

Actually do us a disservice

And instead of bringing us closer as men

Or as brothers in the battle

They actually push us further apart

Shielding us from expressing our feelings

"Who's the closest thing to man in your life cuz?"

"Yuh dad?" "Yuh Mum" "Me?" (laughs)

"Have you ever like, shouted at your son… but winced?… when you saw him flinch?"

"So you're meditating yeah? Wargwarn?"

"Your beard man! It's sick!"

"You know what? I thank god that I've got a brejrin' like you"

In times of need

You're my brother

I love you man

by Richard Wilde

Leo and Cole
by Jake Horowitz

For years Leo imagined this moment, staring out at the lake he knew he'd get married in front of, sensing the summer turn to fall on the breeze, the way only someone born here could. A warmth inside him bloomed with the smell of distant wood smoke. He stared up at the big maple, storing the moment for later in life, and felt the hypnotic pull that the green leaves had when summer was ending. It would only take a few cold days for the tree to turn crimson and gold. A crackling firework show before the wind plucked the leaves and churned the glassy lake into peaks of cold blue icing.

But before all that, marriage to the man he loved. Then a lifetime of watching summer turn to fall, seeing their own summer turn to fall spanning years across from each other at their large, reclaimed oak dinner table. Living.

That's how Leo chose to see it, always the romantic, Cole teased. But as he stood in front of the calm lake, Cole rushing toward him in his tuxedo to ready him for their last photo before marriage, Leo worried that he'd think so hard about the moments coming – the pale green turning into gold – that he'd miss the rest and wake up one winter, cold and alone.

*

Cole hated to see so many strangers trampling through the house he just spent two million dollars on. Did these people – caterers and photographers and a traveling rabbi and a wedding planner (who needed a wedding planner? Not him) – understand that the reindeer hair rug couldn't be cleaned or that the Vera Blanco white porcelain tile in the kitchen still needed to be properly levelled by their lazy contractor?

He took a breath. He was doing this for Leo. Leo, who looked spectacular today in his sheer blue tuxedo with the shawl collar. Leo, whom he'd share this large, quiet home with for a long time to come, each of them finding joy in it in their own way. For Leo, Cole knew, it was the nature of his childhood, the lake he swam in as a kid in the summers, skated on in the winters. For Cole it was the bespoke furnishings he spent two screenplays worth of money on, it was the recessed lighting in the cabinets, the upgradable speakers in the knotted pine ceilings, the hand cut Muskoka granite countertops. But before they could enjoy their favourite separate things together, they needed this photo taken, then they needed to get married.

Cole went outside, found Leo staring at the lake, turned him around and balanced his perfectly messy hair. He took a moment, really trying to force it, to feel it as a memorable moment, to look at his husband to be. Leo was the first man Cole ever dated, and all through their dating he still thought he'd go back to women. He thought their relationship was an entertaining phase, a way to gain experience for an as of yet unwritten script, but years passed and then Cole was just another guy dating a guy. And now here he was getting married. Gay married. To the man he loved.

They smiled into the camera, two men in love. Before the flash Cole thought, is this what my life will be?

*

Leo stared at the photograph, recognizing himself at 29 more than the version of himself that he sees every day in the mirror at 92. The pad of his index finger – lined so deeply he doesn't acknowledge it as belonging to him – strokes the face of Cole. The Cole he remembers. Sitting on the low grey sofa with a blanket over his lap, Leo can't believe he's still in the house where this photo was taken. He can't believe this is it, the rest is gone. The moment with the green leaves that he spent his life remembering is barely real. He wants to shout at the photo. He wants to tell the Cole from the photo, the one he remembers, what his life will become. You'll get successful. More than you are here. You'll leave home to shoot films in exotic locations. You'll leave me here while you sleep with beautiful women. You'll come back, care for me, get old and stare at me. You'll try to work out who I am while I wipe food off your face and give you a kiss on the cheek. You'll forget me, die, leave me alone. In those moments I'll hate you.

But now, forever, I'll love you.

by Hilary Lynch

Bridge Sighs to Soothe City Street
by Simon Engwell

All lines of this poem appearing in italics are based on found words from the Metro newspaper's 'Good Deed Feed' from March, April and May of 2018.

At my head, the railway bridge;
Broken white line on tarmac, my spine
A triangle of green garden at my toes.
My name is Bridge Street.
Glass shop fronts rest in shadow
As the sun rises to fill cross roads.
Cleaners hose damp freshness into air
Mixing with the smell of baked bread.
Young and old emerge from car parks
To shop for food and treats
As the sun warms pavements.
I am a busy but amenable street.

She pushes the trolley to the till.
Makes final check of shopping list.
Child wants sweets and won't sit still.
She searches to find shortest queue;
This one has four people; it will do.
But these are the slowest four;
Others will be quicker out the door.
Child gets bored and starts to bawl.
All look as he pretends to fall.
Shopping placed on the conveyor.
Item by item clocked by blue laser.
Card twice refused; no cash to pay.

Debbie bought my food shopping: I had run
Out of cash. Malawian man and his daughter
Paid parking: I didn't have any coins.

Light is fading to evening.
A young woman on a blanket begging
Her face is drawn and spotted.
A man, stocky frame but skinny,
Approaches, she stands.
They gather together
Their ramshackle bundle.
Down an alley she applies makeup,
In sharp stench of rotting bins.
Turning to tricks to fund a fix
That dulls the pain of a cold night.
She emerges, they walk together,
Waiting for the call.

Bus driver helped attacked and distressed homeless man.
Homeless man selflessly kept fallen elderly lady warm.
Charity thanks homeless man who donated all his change.

Sign in the window says: Private Function.
Beer foams over and prosecco bubbles.
Over the phone: 'the party's at The Junction.'
One girl starts to talk about her troubles;
Her brother consoles her with a cuddle.
At first, single men and women appear meek,
Tongue tied: an awkward muddle.

Drink contrives to help them speak.
Someone lightly slaps a bum, what a cheek.
She waves, starts to make an allegation.
Turns to peer at faces trying to seek…
It's her boyfriend in conversation,
Among a crowd in a state of animation.

*The saint who looked after me when in a very bad
And embarrassing way, I fell over when going from the pub.
I got home safe.*

The rubbish bins are full:
Fast food trays and wrappings
Have over flowed to the floor.
A newspaper page blows down the road.
Down the empty street crawls a police car.
Pubs and bars are unlit but it's not dark.
Street and shop lights still shine
And confused birds sing too early.
It is a warm night
But the stonework cools.
All is calm, and I sigh:
'All will be well.'

The Honey Bees of Syria
by Russell Christie

It was while teaching English in Odessa, Ukraine, that I heard how the most expensive honey is made.

'In the desert, long way in the desert, far from anywhere, far from any flowers, my family have a farm. They grow honey bees there. They make honey. This, this special honey. Please try. Please try, my teacher. It is lemon. Eat it with a spoon.'

We were sitting in a large office in an ornate, nineteenth century building on Pushkin Boulevard. The ceilings of the grand room were high and tall windows overlooked the plane trees of the street. The sound of traffic over cobbles drifted up, muffled and hushed by leaves and by floor to ceiling curtains. Three large desks, pushed together, occupied the room and at the head of them sat Adnan, my student.

'Please try, my teacher.'

In front of me, on a silver tray, was a glass of tea and a small pot of honey, set honey the pale amber of double cream. Adnan looked at me eagerly, perhaps hungry to taste my pleasure vicariously and rekindle a lust that had become jaded with wealth.

I had already learned to take my time with any delicacies that my wealthy students offered. Indeed, with any luxuries that life sent in my direction. Sensuality is everywhere constantly but, as a poor man, the most deeply concentrated forms of physical pleasure are not so frequently available. I knew that this would be one of those rare moments. Through my life there have been ten physical revelations, in relation to food, in which the depth of an experience overwhelms and deepens the knowledge brought to it in perception. At moments like these, I strive to relax, if that is not a contradiction, and attempt to lengthen time into that holding stillness in which every experience becomes a broad, stationary eternity. I deployed the calm I had into the space of the room and let everything in my lived, and as yet un-lived, history lick around the small blue pot of pale, yellow ochre honey and the delicate silver tea-spoon at its side. Adnan became briefly cast with anxiety at my hesitation, as though fearing a negative judgement of the honey.

I sat up squarely on my office chair and leaned toward the silver tray. The damp tannins and mint of the tea drifted toward me, their steam sucked into the currents I made. I took a moment to breathe in this first sensory array. Adnan had not yet fully informed me of the origins of this honey, but I knew the nineteenth century room I was sitting in and I knew Adnan's wealth and something of how he acquired it. Nothing is ever separate from its situation and no perception devoid of the contextual interpretations we bring to it. All gathered now, around this little pot. It is always both what I know and my ignorance that appears in the taste of things, like a gap that experience will fill.

I lifted the well balanced, silver spoon and felt the stiff honey yield as I dipped into the pot. Its stickiness grasped the spoon. I held the small tub and lifted out a mound of pale meringue which sighed as it gave. A moment as everything stopped. And then, the lemon came. A perfume released, its mild notes gliding toward me on a cloud above the tea and mint and then overwhelming the leather of my chair.

'I can smell the lemon,' I said.

I slowly moved the loaded substance beneath my nose and into my mouth. Closed my lips around it. And it melted into a springtime of blossoms. Small petals fell on my tongue and spilled there in crystal lemon, sherbet pools. I saw sun reflected from water in caves of darkness, blue and yellow light on the roof of caverns.

'Good? Is it good?'

I savoured it so he could savour it. Creamy ballerinas danced around my mouth.

'That is excellent, Adnan. Thank you. That is the best honey I have ever tasted.'

He smiled from ear to ear.

'How do they get the lemon so strong?'

'My family has a lemon... a lemon grove!' my forty year old student grinned like a schoolboy. Vocabulary was one of our main points of study and we went through ten words a day.

'Yes a grove, in the desert. Long way in the desert. They put water there so they can control it.'

'Irrigation. They irrigate the desert.'

'Yes, they irrigate the desert, my teacher, long way from anywhere. No flowers, no plants, only the lemon trees that they have. So the bees can only eat from there. All the other plants are taken away. So when the trees are flower in the spring, the bees can only eat from lemon, to collect the food for the honey.'

I sipped my tea to clean my palate for the next teaspoon.

'They have nine hives,' Adnan went on. 'Yes, I learned this word, I studied with my other teacher. The houses that the bees live in, they are called hives. Am I correct?'

'Very good, yes.'

'To begin, there are nine of these houses. But then, what happen?'

'What happens?' I emphasise the 'z' sound.

'What happens? When the flowers end?'

'The blossom.'

'When the blossom finish and there are only the trees? Nowhere to eat! What happen next? Where to go for food?'

'A good question. I've never considered that. I don't know. What happens next, when the blossom finishes?'

'They eat each other!'

'They do what?'

Pleased by my surprise, Adnan continues, patient and deliberate with his English for the lesson: 'To begin, there are nine hives. A lot of lemon trees, a lot of food, in the spring. Happy days!' And I know my student is advising me, ten years his junior, about something more than just the processes of honey. The advice he gives is part of his patronage, I accept it with grace, like the twenty dollars, U.S., he pays me an hour. But there is a knock at the office door.

'Come!' says Adnan. The oak door is pushed open and it is Alonya, Adnan's head of kitchen. She carries more tea in an ornate silver pot, and more honey. 'Put it on the table here,' Adnan says, still in English, and then - laughing to me at the humour of his mistake - repeats the instruction in Russian. Alonya places the teapot precisely between us. She is both cheerful and stern, taking life both lightly and heavily.

'But then! Nothing to eat! So what do they do, the nine hives?' Adnan continues his story while Alonya is still in the room. He looks at me.

I pull a dumbfounded face.

'The bees steal each other honey, they attack. Kill the other bees. Eat their honey. The farmer, he do nothing. Sometimes some sugar water, on a plate, not too much, keep them going. The strong bees, they kill the weak bees, eat their honey, bring it to their houses. Nine hives, then seven. Five. In the end: Three hives. These three bees eat the other houses, eat the honey and make it again in their places. This is how it is made. Three times the bees eat and make again. Three times other bees die, extinct. More and more lemon each time. It is good, no?'

I taste again the hoarded sweetness of the honey and nod at its cost.

Adnan was a small, modest man, gently rotund, with slicked back hair and a pleasant smile. He always wore a collared shirt. He was impeccably hospitable and polite. He'd been born to a wealthy Syrian family and had come to Ukraine twenty years before to study at the university of Odessa. He'd settled down in Ukraine as a way of avoiding army service, then compulsory for all young men in Syria. After studying, he met a local woman, got married and started a family. He tried his hand at several businesses, underwritten by money from back home and within the allowances of the communist state, but they failed. Then came Perestroika. By the time of the privatisation of the assets of the Soviet, Adnan had made useful contacts. He had graced his way through the political hierarchy to the position of deputy secretary of the Syrian Communist Party in Ukraine. He was therefore well placed to take advantage of the opportunities that arose during the return of state assets to the people.

I often wondered about the exact process by which my student had made his money. The broad mechanics of it were later laid bare in the book *Putin's Russia*, by Anna Politskaya, describing this time of oligarchs and their acquisitions. For writing this book, the Western orthodoxy is, Politskaya was assassinated, possibly on the orders of Putin. I am still surprised that Adnan, always eager for compliments and reassurance, sitting just across the desk from me, could have been involved in those sternly leveraged buyouts, when Russia and Ukraine became the Wild East. And yet, Adnan did now employ twelve bodyguards, accompanying him and his family day and night. And he had a revolver in the drawer of his desk which he showed me once, out of the blue. Although he himself seemed far too soft and withdrawing a person to ever use it, his right hand man, and a constant presence, was Nickolai. Kolya, to use the diminutive, which I never did. 'Sabaka!' he had hissed one day, under his breath, when I pointed out to the monthly cashier that I'd been given a pay raise: 'Dog!' Nickolai Victorovich Kuznetsov had been a sergeant in the Soviet army, training new recruits in Cuba. He was a hard man, a man who had killed men. I could smell that as keenly as I could smell the mint in the tea on the desk in front of me or the iron in spilled blood.

So Adnan had purchased most of the steel mills of Ukraine during privatisation, cheaply buying up the shares that had been distributed to the workforce of each mill, who knew nothing of stocks and shares and dealing. His agents would ply the mill workers with vodka and then offer them fifty dollars for the paperwork they had recently received. My student then stripped and exported all the assets of the mills to Syria or, via old Soviet connections, to Soviet supported governments in Africa. The steel from the yard, the foundry equipment, ultimately the land, were sold off in order to realise a profit on his investments. I heard reports that he had made fifty million dollars in five years, all entirely legally. The mill workers were now out of work and there was mass unemployment in those dog days of Ukraine.

'It's good, no?' he asked again, bringing me back to the honey, as if I'd left it. I realise now, he was looking to me for more than just vicarious pleasure, more than just the intensity of the flavour of the honey flown in from Syria. He was looking for absolution for the surviving bees. These processes for the acquisition of honey were natural, acceptable, he wanted me to say, the nature of the world.

I sipped my tea to clean my palate for the next teaspoon of bitter lemons.

'It is the best honey I have ever tasted,' I said. It was. I gave him absolution. He was paying me twenty dollars an hour. He had a gun in his desk. And yes, I was involved too, it was also me, his teacher, in those dark windowed, black Mercedes, watched by the people of the city, speeding over the cobbled streets, chauffeured to his lessons when he called me, to honey, to sturgeon in green butter and to caviar.

Now, twenty years later, and long back in England, I watch the news from Syria. I wonder if Adnan is still in Odessa and I imagine the conversations we might have: about 9/11, about the civil war ravaging the country he again cannot return to, about Putin's annexation of Crimea. I wonder what has happened to the lemon groves and to the honey bees. And I wonder if the farmer is still there, the one who laid down the plate of sugared water to keep it all going. The depth of the honey, the tannin of the tea, the mint of the steam, the blood of the world, these swirl in every mouthful of life.

by Hilary Lynch

Tallaahi (I swear by God)
by Taiwo Oyenola

A spoken word/poem written from the perspective of a Muslim who falls in love and tries to understand himself through this experience.

Tallaahi, in my eyes, she is from the most
beautiful that the sun has ever risen over
And from the most elegant upon whom it could
ever set
To have met
A women who kept
Her heart pure
And secure
From the trials of this life
And the burdens of its strife
And with regret
I failed to get
To the level that she's on
That level she rose upon
Or to be
More than what I am
But I can
Do so much better
Because before I even met her
My aims and objectives were there
So clear
Unshaken nor smeared
And it's rare
To meet someone in whom your heart finds

tranquillity
Serenity
And it feels like it was meant to be
She was meant for me
Even though I don't deserve her
I've been reserved for her
Just seeing her, to take one glance
It's like I fall into a trance
Daydreaming in a field of plants
I have to prepare myself in advance
Rearrange my stance
Because it could be my chance
To make her dance
Inside with happiness and joy
The way I enjoy
Her company as a priceless jewelled treasure
And pleasure
Without measure
And to gaze
Into the rays
Of her hazel eyes
Underlies
The bliss I'm gazing at two pearls of paradise
It's the presence
it's like everything else fades
And degrades
Into the shades
Of the blades
Of grass
Cast far from reality

Completely irrelevant
Gone
It's this moment that's prevalent
Benevolent
Of the highest grade
But I was made
To obey
ALLAH
So I turn away
Walk away stay away
It's like a fight
But it's her right
That I don't look her touch her
Let alone hug at her
She's not for me to see
But Inshallah she will be
Until then
I just plant the seeds
The seeds of affection in her heart
Towards me right from the start
Rooted firmly so it can't be torn apart

Watered by my tears to Allah by night and day
Asking Him to keep me away
From haram
And to calm
The thoughts of doubt
And remove the clout
That stops me from seeing the possibility that she could be my wife
Forever in this life

And the next
On thrones
Awaiting the promised gaze

by Richard Wilde

ALONELY
by Matthew Healing

They could sit there for days and go mad,
suspended on a perch above the world
They would caw down and brief some wandrin'
passer-by in conversation
Lucid enough and lonely enough to entertain
those mad wonderings
Though they've been shooed many a time, and
whistled off down lurid streets
With a spastic tune to fit the frightful night
I find fatigue sets in the second I've stepped out,
into that wild dark
It makes me want to stay in, bright the hallways
and dim the bedroom
Become a present spectre in a haunted house,
peering from that sill
Cigarette in hand, I struggle to tell us apart
That cold dark pebbling the window, beckoning
to the time-travelled child
To wake me too abruptly from that fetid dream
Calling to the time-travelled child, its reality is
the sill
Its perch is a field, and its space is all, enough

A Broken Deck
by Macauley Raymond Foster

'Pick a card.'

You caught my eye as you entered the fête. You're small, for six. You stared longingly at the candyfloss machine by the entrance. You don't even want the sugar but food's food, right? I fan out the cards before you. 'They're all the same,' I add with a wink. You don't catch the joke and your mum don't care, but it doesn't matter. I've already decided you'll pick the Three of Clubs.

That's my favourite card, and you're bending it a little as you stare at Penn Jillette's signature. I waited an hour in line to get it autographed and I fight to keep my smile fixed as you smush the corner pushing it back into the deck.

I pretend to read your mind. The usual spiel. Imagine a canvas equidistance between us and project your card onto it... Your mother taps her foot impatiently.

'Is it a black card?' I say. 'Yes, of course,' I add before you can reply.

You smile. You believe me. For a second, I believe me. I almost say, 'The smile confirms it,' or some crap about microexpressions.

But I don't. I don't need to lie to you. I don't need to lie to me.

Anyway, I don't need to read your mind. I can read your face. Your card's plastered all over it, heavy as the foundation you're half a decade too young to wear.

You shouldn't hide it. Kids run into shit, catch black eyes, all the time. That's what your mum said, right?

I tug my shirtsleeve further over my wrist. At least you have someone else to hurt you.

Amidst the foundation I see the Three of Clubs but also all the clubs your mum spends all night in.

I camp up the flourish a bit too much. Your mother sneers at me, at the twist in my wrist, the flamboyant flick of my fingers as I produce the card from nowhere. I glance at her. *Gay*, she's thinking. *Faggot*, I'm thinking. I tug my sleeve fully over the meat of my thumb, shake my head clear.

You're laughing. Been a while, hasn't it? I join you, and for the first time in a week I'm not forcing it. I vanish the card and you cry *Bring it back!*

You're mad.

You were mad at your mum too, when she made your brother vanish. When the black car pulled up and he disappeared inside of it. You tried to chase it down the street. *Bring it back!* but she never did.

Vanishing something is easy.

Don't worry.

I point at your hip.

You slip a hand into your tatty cardigan. Your face lights up. You find the card, and also a Mars bar because that's really the best I can do. Your mother grips your shoulder. You flinch.

'Did you touch my daughter?' She's mad too, you know. At me. At your dad. At you.

'It's a trick.' I shrug as straightly as I can. 'Thanks, mister!' you cry before your mother drags you off. You're clutching the card. You think it's my own signature, a souvenir. That card's priceless to me, but it's okay. I won't take anything away from you.

Back at the flat, sitting up against the cold radiator with caramel between your teeth, you'll look at the card and the wonder will make you feel like a real kid again, for a moment.

Vanishing something is easy. A mercury fold. A palm. An argument. Hard part's bringing it back.

Your mother snatches the half-open chocolate bar from your hand, throws it into the grass. 'Don't take food from strangers,' she says, even though dinner last night was a handful of cold chips you found on the ground outside the club.

I stretch my jaw, force myself not to wince as I scratch at my wrist.

I shuffle the broken deck, palm a chocolate bar, and wait for the next kid.

Pink Petals
by Mark O'Loughlin

Concrete coloured suburban skies.
A tube journey before I walk.

No more car stereo or open window,
I listen to them talk.

The two men eat broken biscuits from an H&M bag.
I cannot understand what they say.

Green fields give way to graffiti on warehouse facades.
Chimneys and naked trees fill the sky.

Passengers get on and on and on and the two men get off.
Micro flats replace major houses, balconies replace gardens.

Two more stops to go before gaps of violent blue poke between the clouds,
birds are singing as though noticing the premature pink petals for the first time.

by Jacqueline Chesta

How To Be A Good Spy
by Lia Courtenay Harlin

I'm stood in line at the bank to finally pay off the last of my loan. I took it out, cor, about, six years ago now for a trip to Disneyland. My daughter and I were both adults when we made it but we loved every second of it. Best holiday ever.
I go to the cashier, "I'd like to pay 160 pounds, please."

She types it in and I'm like, going on about how relieved I am to have that all out the way now and we start chatting about ideas for ours next holiday plans and she recommends me Centre Parcs. Then I reach in my bag, pull out my purse and there's only sixty quid inside. For as long as I can remember we've been poor: council housing on a council estate, benefits, channels 1-5 instead of freeview, then freeview instead of sky, being stuck looking up at England's grey sky while everybody else gets blue. No matter how many extra hours I took on we never had any money and it drove me insane, you know? There never seemed to be enough leftover at the end of the week to get my nails done or go for a night out. I slam the purse shut and look behind me embarrassed.

"Silly cow, I must have left it at home. What am I like?" I say. "Sorry about that."

"Oh! Not a problem at all. See you later," she smiles. I smile. And then I turn my back.

I'd been looking for a new job for about a year now with no luck, and I finally got one...as a spy (but don't tell anyone). Now I've worked tonnes of jobs in my lifetime: cleaning, admin, bar work, retail but this has to be the most exhausting one so far. You've gotta constantly be on the ball, day and night. I never signed up for it, it just happened over time. Life had been going by at a tortoise pace since my daughter left home so now I have time to actually take in everything around me. I could hear him sniffling in the bathroom at night for long periods of time. I'd hear him on the phone agreeing to meet someone, a woman's voice. I'd ask him who it was and he'd say,

"Just me boss." Like you work as a fucking builder, there ain't any women in your workplace!

When my daughter, Amy was back for a weekend she caught one of the skanky neighbours pacing the front of our house late at night, and he kept trying to sneak out to meet her. He'd say "I'm just popping to the shop babes" and not come back for an hour. Sometimes he'd come home without a shopping bag at all, the knobhead. Amy stopped visiting home. She said we were always bickering over the smallest things and she couldn't take it anymore. I looked back at all the things I'd overlooked: the spoilt birthdays, trips to the zoo, winter wonderland, we even got into a tiff at Disneyland because he didn't want to watch the fireworks. Who the fuck doesn't want to watch the fucking fireworks at fucking Disneyland? Miserable sod. I remembered how miserable *she* was on our wedding day and I'd put it down to her being a stroppy teenager. I didn't see how unsupportive he was when my Mum was sick. I didn't see that rapidly receding hairline, the bank account decline, the growing alcohol consumption.

But now I've worked out how to be a good spy.

To avoid random things going missing like Christmas cards or airport money from your daughter's room, you need to be better at hiding things than they are. Thankfully I've had years of practice from hiding Christmas presents from a curious child. My Dad is coming round today so I hide all the blankets from the sofa. I've become a master at hiding my feelings.

"Everything's fine, yeah, yeah, everything's great!" I say, putting the kettle on with a smile.

"How's the job search coming along?" asks Dad.

"Still nothing," I reply, taking out the 'best daughter' mug Dad got me for my last birthday.

Number two: you also need to be great at finding things like unpaid bills tucked under sofa cushions or condom wrappers in trouser pockets.

"You'll find something soon. I know it. Everything happens for a reason," assures Dad, leaning on the counter. "Where's Simon?"

Number three: you have to be great at making and recognising excuses.

"Hard at work," I say. He's not at work. He reckons he's been at work for the past week doing extra late shifts, but he's left and come home without his work clothes on and I found them folded up in the car, smelling freshly washed.

There's a knock at the door.

"Is Simon home?" I don't recognise the man.

"He's at work, he won't be back til late," I say.

"Oh. Just tell him it's Craig from football. He said I could borrow some old weights for a bouncy castle party next week."

"Right." So, of course, I text Simon and ask him who Craig is. *Apparently,* Craig is an old colleague who wants him to do some extra work but he doesn't pay well. *Apparently,* all the texts on his phone I found asking for "a small bit" were from a hacker. *Apparently.* the messages where he owed people money were a bunch of gypsies who owned a van of stolen clothes that Simon got mixed up in somehow. *Apparently,* the packet of white powder I found in his pocket was simply "a sample of asbestos" from work.

"Poor Simon, I heard about him getting paid less at work. Seems so unfair to judge him on one simple mistake," sighs Dad, taking a sip of coffee.

"Oh, he told you about that?" I heard his boss wasn't paying him at all.

"Yeah. Then what with the stolen van. You two aren't having much luck these past few months." Oh yeah, the company van was nicked, but also taken away from him because of a road rage incident.

"Let's put our heads together and think up some job ideas. Are you good with numbers? I heard there's some accounting jobs going at-" Numbers. That's an essential skill to spy work. I've become an expert at counting the amount of trips he takes to the shops every night and counting how many beers he gets through. I'm constantly monitoring my bank accounts to make sure money doesn't disappear whenever I blink. I keep track of all the bills he says he's paid and add up the speeding and parking fines he racks up. I've gotta work out how much he underpays me for his share of rent and the changing numbers of how much he reckons he owes people.

"What about being a carer? You're patient and caring-"

"I'm not being a carer." I already deal with enough shit. Living with someone else I have to monitor every second of the day? I've asked him to leave but he refuses to go; his name's on the lease, he says he has nowhere to go but he won't even speak to his family to ask. And I can't afford to keep this place on my own so I have to grin and bear it until I find a full-time job.

"What other skills would you say you have?" asks Dad. I'm exceptionally skilled at pretending. I pretend to be asleep when he tries to snuggle into bed to hug me. I pretend I'm not married. My online dating profile says single and my ring is hidden in the house like his stash. I'm surprised he hasn't sold that yet. I'm pretending to my own parent that everything's fine because I don't want to worry him. And because I'm too proud. Not that there's anything I can do about it anyway. He won't go to marriage counselling, he won't go to AA, he won't admit he has a problem, so he won't quit. So I have my little secrets too.

I pretend to care when I find condom packets in his pockets. The only reason I do care is because it's probably nicked from my box. I pretended to be into mountain climbing to join a hiking club just to get a chance at mounting one of the men. I hate heights. But a good spy is always in good physical shape and gets laid on the regular.

He read an article about them making the next James Bond a woman, and he went off on one, about how women can't this and women can't that. A good spy is stealthy. This morning I used the iron to steam open one of his old bills. I have that Mum talent of always being able to find something that's lost. Like his stash of coke he hides in the barbeque outside. With my delicate, lady hands I opened the packet and poured the coke down the bog bowl. I crushed up some cat litter and replaced it with that and slipped it back into the barbeque.

"I'm not good at anything," I say, taking a sip from my "best daughter" mug.

by Thomas Ryan

Uxbridge? Is that London?
by Connor Smith

Every time when I get home from Brunel,
My friends ask the same thing, it's a living hell.
They always ask "Brunel? Who?"
I explain "It's in Uxbridge!", but they've no clue
"Uxbridge? Is that London?", their brains in mayhem
And this is what I have to tell them.
It's like London, but not London
And the likeness is abundant.
We have Maccies and a Nando's
The ever-growth of London is what that foreshadows.
Pushing out and out its Tarmac boundary,
Crisp fields cast into its iron foundry.
It's like the capital, but not the capital.
It is and isn't just as admirable.
"Stones throw away from central?" That's just rude!
It's actually a whole hour on the tube.
And the trains stench is hot and thick,
It clings like a burrowed Tic.
It's like the city, but not the city.
It can be sublime but also quite gritty.
There's the murmuration of sloths on shopping safaris,
But they're more alert than the 'Zone 1 Zombies'.
Aimlessly shopping as the day goes by,
And right in the way they stop. Why?!

It's like central, but not central.
The similar price of beer isn't coincidental.
Six pounds fifty for a Kebab,
Plus an extra seven in the cab.
Just as much money is spent on meat
From this Uxbridge to Baker Street.
It's like The Big Smoke, but not The Big Smoke.
The same littered air serves to choke.
Cars clump together to make a road clog
And still there's the same polluted smog.
See that's the problem felt everywhere,
The slow infection of our dying air.

Spinning Time
by Adam Johnson

There's a steel saucepan on the kitchen counter. It's been there since Saturday, last Saturday that is, and new life is growing in the bottom, green and spongey. I would move it, clean it even, but I am sat down at the kitchen table and it does not belong to me. So, it's a permanent exhibit in the museum of irresponsibility. There are plenty of other examples dotted around. The chicken wings burnt to charcoal, displayed on a baking tray upon the stove which, now you mention it, is dusted with crumbs. To the left, beneath the cupboards, a selection of tea bags, green, earl grey, Lidl gold, untouched in their boxes, and a pot painted yellow, filled with soggy brown carcasses, the casualties of teas drank a few months back. To the left and behind me, we have the centre piece of this collection. The fridge that has never been cleaned. It will not be opened, not for more than three seconds, at the risk of passing out from the unique smell. And I am shuffling playing cards. They're wrinkled, scars received from drunken nights when spillages cannot be avoided. The cards are from Russia, a gift from my sister and they depict iconic landmarks of Moscow instead of the usual King, Queen or Jack. Unfortunately, every picture looks like the Kremlin.

The window opposite me is like a long horizontal crack in the wall, just above the two blocked sinks, and coming through is a warm orange light. The sun is setting, and I haven't left halls today. By my calculations, my skin has not been kissed by its rays in three days, I haven't washed in two, and my last meal was yesterday at four-thirty, officially the most peculiar time of day to eat.

There's not a muscle in my body that wants to move but, at this point, a flat mate walks in. I am relieved to see that he is also wearing pyjamas. A tuft of hair at his crown stands upright. With all the evidence before me, I am confident in my belief that he has just woken up and think smugly to myself that I had the tenacity to be out of bed by three in the afternoon.

'You wanna go out?' I grunt.
The sudden appearance of this flat mate has spurned me into productivity.

'Huh?'

The response does not fill me with confidence. His eyes haven't focused yet. Give him time.

'I haven't been outside in three days, I'm practically a vampire so-'

The flat mate has wandered behind me, wisely avoiding the fridge, and heads for the vat of mystery that is the saucepan.

'How long has that been there?' he asks.
'Sorry?'
'The pot of despair,' he bravely lifts the pot by its handle to draw my attention, but immediately

thinks otherwise and it clatters into the sink, 'Jesus fu- how long has that been there?'

'I don't know.'

'That is fucking disgusting.'

'So, do you want to go out?'

I watch his eyes refocus again. They are bloodshot, I think he's been smoking. His movements are slow, thoughtful.

'Sure.'

'Yeah?'

'Sure. Let's go somewhere.'

Excellent, I am galvanised. I abandon the cards. A plan has been formed. At six o'clock in the evening I am going outside with a friend. Now I have a purpose. I say: 'Great. Get dressed, and meet back here in fifteen?'

It's efficient. He nods, I leave the kitchen through the door behind me to the left, wisely avoiding the fridge, and I stride down the hallway. It's a murky darkness, the sensor for the light malfunctioned after a lightning storm we experienced last month, and it still hasn't been fixed. No one has emailed maintenance yet. My room is number seven. As I enter, the safety hinge at the top of the door scrapes the adjacent wall, leaving a deep, paint-scratched groove. It's broken. I haven't emailed maintenance yet. The room itself I I'd rather not go into detail, but I gather a selection of outside appropriate clothing from the floor and leave, ready to convince the world I am a high functioning adult. I proceed to wait twenty-five minutes in a semi-black hallway for my stoned flatmate to change out of his penguin pyjama onesie.

My room is number seven. As I enter, the safety hinge at the top of the door scrapes the adjacent wall, leaving a deep, paint-scratched groove. It's broken. I haven't emailed maintenance yet. The room itself I'd rather not go into detail, but I gather a selection of outside appropriate clothing from the floor and leave, ready to convince the world I am a high functioning adult. I proceed to wait twenty-five minutes in a semi-black hallway for my stoned flatmate to change out of his penguin pyjama onesie.

We leave our Halls and we begin walking with no sense of destination, following our aimless feet. The sun has all but disappeared. There are pale street lamps at intervals of around forty to fifty feet down the campus street, a fake street that has been empty for the last three weeks except for any other rambling pairs and groups rather shamelessly still in their pyjamas. Their conversations, like ours, are stilted. We cover topics spoken about on previous hikes, and we attempt to recover them again, like trying to breathe life into a dusty old croon. We are not listening to each other, except for the occasional grunt. I don't mind. I didn't come out for the conversation nor for the scenery. I also don't mind feeling this way because I know my flat mate feels it too. We simply desire the companionship.

Whilst we keep up the disinterested exchange of food shops and Marvel movies and stale dramas between campus friends, the secret truth in our minds is we are both petrified. We wear the dark-eyed look of sleepless uncertainty. It is the look on the face of every rambler we pass on this wide road as it moves with lethargic bends through campus. Behind our tired eyes we are hyper aware. We stand on the very brink of our education and stretching before us is the bleak frontier of the rest of our lives. We don't speak a word of our minds. We communicate through long pauses, worried glances and grimaces, and excessive laughter following mediocre jokes. We continue to walk and walk and we walk ourselves back to where we started, like hamsters on a wheel, spinning away the time. We return to the kitchen at half past one in the morning, satisfied. Today, we achieved something, and we reward ourselves with Captain America on the biggest laptop screen, sharing a tub of ice cream between us.

When The Party's Over
by Vivien Brown

When I was young they strapped me in a chair
and fed me pureed fruit from sticky spoons.
I dribbled, got it tangled in my hair,
laughed at bubbles, screamed at popped
balloons.
My mother'd made a cake shaped like a two.
My father's hand struck matches on a box.
And in the darkness everybody blew,
while I fidgeted, and fiddled with my socks.
Unsteady legs, high-sided plastic bed,
bottom cleaned; the guests all disappeared.
A lidded cup to suck as father said,
'At least that's over for another year.'
Life's circle turns. The candles burn anew
now I am old, and drenched in déjà vu.

The Sister
by Aisling Lally

Up until the age of six
Every birthday candle wish
Would be for your very own
Baby sister

Your wish came true,
'She's nice' you said
Awe and wonder filled your head
You leaned over the hospital bed
And whispered to me,
'Hi, sister'

I was in hospital for four days straight
Plus I came over three weeks late
Not perfect no, but a 'little gem'
Your every own, sister

We didn't always play perfectly,
Like the time I stamped on your foot
with such force
That you bled and still, I showed no remorse
You snubbed my colouring, so I stubbed your
toe, what else could I do, big sister?

But playtime ends and lessons begin,
And the toughest I ever learnt was how,
You got older and colder, didn't want me now,
Well, you didn't want anyone, sister.

You'd shout and scream,
You'd shriek and roar
Caught mum's fingers in the door,
I saw every bruise, I heard every cry,
Alone in my room, hopelessly wondering why,
A storm had wrecked our game
of happy families,
A storm in the shape of you, sister.

Have you ever wondered what it was like?
Me coming from school not knowing
If you'd be alive?

My *grades* would thrive,
1:25am.
Parties, alcohol, vomit, fun.
2:25am
Singing lessons.
3:25am
Smiled when necessary.
4:25am
The word horrid carved into your arm.
5:25am
Netball practice.
6:25am
Play rehearsals.
7:25am
Repeat.

Your little gem lost her spark
With all your pain, every vicious remark
When I reached for your arm
and saw a new mark
I'm side lined and silent,
muffling tears in the dark
Where the fuck did you go, big sister?

And if I could take each pulsation of pain
That throbs on your body, inside and out
If I could I take it all for you, without a shout,
I would in a heartbeat, sister.

It's not just the sufferers that suffer
For the sister sometimes it feels tougher.

Up until the age of sixteen
Every birthday candle wish
Would be for the long awaited return
Of my very own, big sister.

by Jacqueline Chesta

The Pregnant Afternoon
by Luke Buffini

This afternoon is a premonition. It is a vision of the dark, magnificent story about to be told of an evening and a night. I will watch it through this office window.

Slowly and inexorably, the furniture of afternoon will loosen and release its grip on me, floating upwards and dropping into the black ocean of evening. Everything before me now, each name and phrase which comprises the afternoon, is also a line in the prologue of the evening.

I hear the age of birds ending. This is my first clue. The music is gone, leaving only a solitary songbird, hidden within the labyrinth of branches and twigs that compose the Conifer outside. He wails out his eulogy for his brothers, who jostle around in the fuss of departing. A brave, final testament to elegance, offered up to the silent sky.

This English summer is hot and short. The short, hot months are squashing together to make long, hot days and the people are draining all the life out of them. My feeling of anticipation is all the more intense and vivid because of this. There is more time and light to watch the approaching evening fulfil itself than in winter or autumn or spring. A mature hour like 5 o'clock, for instance, can paint its face with the makeup of the afternoon sky, affecting the appearance of an hour much younger than itself. Yet the evening is still being born much the same: the evening actors are still playing their parts and the afternoon is only dying a little slower…

It sinks a little more into the evening when the children finish playing. The afternoon is their theatre and they play across every inch of it. Different scenes form the same drama spread out across streets, gardens, parks and in cars. Each actor utterly engrossed in the person they are creating. They are ecstatic because every tomorrow is a new costume, and there are more tomorrows than can be counted. The atmosphere of evening rises out of their exit. The play ends without applause. The sky is almost ready to let down its dark curtain.

The omen in the afternoon is bound up inextricably with all of London's young people. They feel it on their skin; they flirt with it. It is rediscovered every summer by those pub and park creatures who dare to begin celebrating earlier and earlier in the day. One day in June, they tiptoe out into the streets at 3pm. All seems well. So, a few days later, perhaps they try their luck at 1pm. They are perplexed –can life really be this generous? Their perpetual festival is given a new and strange quality as the afternoon levitates higher and higher in the day. Grape and grain and music seem to be enhanced by certain, earlier hours. Some indecipherable expectation swells the souls and organs of these young men and women. They have an eagerness – perhaps even a trust – that unlimited euphoria is to be offered them this very day. This city is deluged, swollen and ready to burst with anticipation. The cricket green in Ealing is ripe and the riverside pub benches in Hammersmith are plump. The high-ceilinged drinking houses in Notting Hill are brimming and the first spillages of an overflowing summer trickle down the thin cobbled streets of Richmond-upon-Thames.

In London, there is an expression for this anxiousness for joy. They would say: 'this day is pregnant'. Perhaps the most alluring hallmark of youth is excitement. The instant connectivity available in our era only exacerbates this. Long, dull office hours are combated by a constant stream of texts describing the facile indulgences to come at the hour of liberty. Often, the indulgences themselves are irrelevant. Not that these indulgences aren't noteworthy themselves. The ease with which these young men and women slide into laughter and sensuality once they are beyond the office walls demonstrates an appetite for happiness which is worth recording here. But that 'pregnant' feeling really represents an excitement about nothing in particular – in other words, about everything. The premonition in the afternoon, embodied by the fluttering and hopping impatience of youth, is a symptom of an enormous desire for all of life and its constant joys.

The evening rises. The Sun sinks. It half-paints the faces of trees and makes them ruggedly handsome; it grins between the brick chimneys and gilds rooftops in coats of gold. Clouds clasp around it and it puckers open on the horizon. Soon, the afternoon prophesises, that bright mouth shall close, the lip of the sky shall meet the lip of the horizon, pressing together firmly, poising to blow breath after breath of darkness across the world. The trees stand proud and undaunted as their lifeblood drains from their faces. All that life-giving light washes out of the sky on the tide of evening and finally circles the drain at the horizon.

The Sun reaches the bottom step of the sky and my mind transforms. I am granted a seat amongst all the great poets of the past. In that corner of the sky, the Sun leaves a furious, burning signature. The afternoon drives off over the horizon and tosses a few memorable photographs out of the window. In these images are presented all the misunderstandings and superstitions of man in his infancy. There is something irrationally frightening in the beauty of nature. Our fascination and horror of it, at once so nourishing and negating, has made us make humans out of it. Or, at least, demi humans. Man's own power of perception, burning his eyes and convulsing his mind, relinquished timidly to unworthy gods.

The turn of the evening is a perfect moment. The belly of the afternoon, fat with the evening, splits and the whole thing collapses and tumbles. London is the same, but changed. It's the darkness that changes her – darkness changes everything. The silence bloats at first. Those who only glance at it get the impression of waiting for something to happen. Everything is set. A warm, black rug rolled out from horizon to horizon, the boards of the earth swept clean and bare, their nakedness spotlighted by the silver moon. Children are put to bed with their superstitions: naive eyes see monsters in the dark.

If you don't think it, you don't see it. It requires only a single line of thought, and yet without that the entire story is missed. It is happening right now. The evening roared in like a herd of black horses as I watched. Tomorrow I might not even notice. But today, I have watched things change. The sky, in its new black and sequined dress, is luring a new mood out of London. With the curtains drawn, the whole place begins to throb with the ecstasy of freedom in its youth. There is an affair happening. In these narrow streets, beneath these dirty club ceilings, at tables in shiny restaurants and outside old pubs, there is an affair happening between people and their freedom.

Driving the A40 home, a huge sky sits on the flat horizon. The buildings and cranes have been rolled up and tucked away. This motorway is a hallway to the sky. On this long, empty spine there is nothing else to fill my eyes. Here, the shade of the evening announces itself as a regal blue and green. Refined and magisterial, this colour fills my vision right up to the very corners. All my eyes are the sky. My mind is the sky. I see something whole. I understand something complete. This enigmatic ceiling in front of me exists now and only now. It will not exist tomorrow morning, and I will never rediscover the feeling it just gave me – that unique texture of feeling. This evening sky will die, buried and inscribed with my naked awe of it. Who will mourn this broad jewel of the evening?

My heart beats against my chest. A great wooden door being rapped on. I feel sick and I let the hot evening air in through the window. My car is very small, and I am smaller within it. The road turns. The road swings round and I turn the car, turning my stomach with it.

I'm around the bend and here is another canvas of the sky crowning me. My regal evening jewel is gone – a lost artefact somewhere behind the bend, behind now. And yet here is something new and distinct. Just a few short minutes on, one mile further, here is an entirely new pocket of the heavens.

Not the *heavens*. Heaven – the horrible totality of the idea disgusts me. This is not heaven, but something more beautiful, briefer and less human. The sky is not human. Heavens and nirvanas – these are human inventions. Stony eternities and uniform bliss –preferences of the incurious and submissive mind.

This sky...this sky which has already shed its evening skin and is now glittering like a black, scaled dragon. This restless sky. Clouds hurrying across, frantically preparing the scene change before lights up at dawn. Not yet black, not yet empty, this sky is a cosmic blueberry.

My laughter surges up through the silence. I nod – absurdly – as if to acknowledge what the sky is showing me. The sky: which has shown me nothing; and I: laughing with tears in my eyes. I am ridiculous and alone. But so too is this beauty ridiculous. Ridiculous and doomed.

There is an abundance of secrets hidden in the night. The night sky should forever be the image of human freedom. The idea that at any place, in any era, anyone can look up and see a star-sprinkled slice of the darkness that covers us all. At any moment, I can reach up and carve something for myself from that infinite banquet of the eyes, and of the mind. Each piece I take is different from the last, and though someone else may also take on the same night as I, they take something entirely distinct.

In the past, those who came with blunt instruments to carve answers from the night departed still hungry. They looked up and saw monsters and gods; they saw the wrath of Apollo or Helios in the absence of the sun and felt guilty; they gouged out the stars and put eyes in and felt reassured by their own fear. To the moon they gave the power to corrupt, and they blamed it when things went foul. Most of the people that have lived before now have suffered an irrational amount of fear, guilt, shame and disgust because of this glimmering ceiling.

I have feared this dark. Even god-slayers fear the dark. Expelling those dictators of the sky leaves a fear vacuum, which the god-slayer sucks up in his mouth. I might not see gods anymore, but I still imagine monsters in the dark. Faceless, shapeless monsters. I breathe my fear into the nothingness and give it life. I make a villain of the dark – its oppression is silence; its wrath is its ignorance of me. Man makes a monster of his independence. He feels his freedom is something to be feared. Trying to shake himself into action, he gives the imposing trait of boundlessness to his freedom. He makes the freedom of the night a bottomless ocean, and he fears he might fall in.

But my infinite freedom is another fictitious nirvana. Eternal dark, like eternal light, is another spell of man's petrification. I can indulge myself in notions of my limitless freedom, and I will never act for fear of wasting it. Others entertain themselves with the idea of eternal bliss in the next life, and they too will never act since they are already promised everything. Man needs his boundaries – big ones, to be sure – to live within.

The calm premonition, the sacrifice of the afternoon, the rise of a muscular and pulsating evening, and black night – all inextricably woven together. It's the greatest child's play:

unwatched, unsupervised and entirely improvised, the naive actors stomp across the stage, pound their chests and spin in lucid reverie. Behind the curtain, no applause will come, they know this, and they dance on all the more furiously.

Death is bewildered into silence by the defiance of this dance. The beat which London strums out into the night sky is a song of life. Rather like the eulogy of the birds amidst the eroding afternoon; these people, my people, stand in the ruins of the day and screech out an epilogue. They sing together and they say that tomorrow they shall build it all back up again, just to watch it stand, sway and tumble down once more. The night sky, if it observes this, is unmoved.

by Richard Wilde

Sometimes I Hear Them
by Iris Hontiveros Mauricio

When the warbirds start to sing, I'll be gone.
No note, just the sound of the door clicking shut,
a space for you to find someone else
to fill in again.
A photo left on the mantle we used to share:
A cliff. The ocean. You.
One eye squinted against the sun.

I had a dream of you taking an axe
to the base of a tree,
hacking at its roots, ripping them from the
ground with your bare hands
when you had to. I woke up and stared at the
outline of your body in the dark,
an island at the edge of the bed that
I thought I knew.

I tried to ask you once who your mother was.
If she had your eyes, your hands.
Your rigid smile.
I wanted the image of you as a child, loving.
Being loved.
You didn't answer. Just threw a stone into the
pond in our garden,
watched the ripples stretch outwards like sonar.
That night, you crawled into bed,
curled away from me. Went to sleep.

I remember that the needles in your words
always took me by surprise,
because you were gentle, like dusk light, like the
sky at night, and then you weren't.
Always sudden. Always no note, and the sound
of the door clicking shut.
Then you at the cliff,
dangling your legs over the edge.

I thought I heard the warbirds today,
but it was just you.
Just your voice carried in
by the returning summer.
The back of my shirt darkened with sweat
as I packed my bags.
I took your picture from the mantle. Put it back.
Closed all the curtains
but left the windows open.

The Enemy Within
by Lorraine Collins

Julia   April 2018

Dear Sally

I'm so sorry I haven't been in touch for ages, and I didn't even send the usual Christmas update. I know you're hurt by my silence, so I thought I'd write now as so much (and in a way, so little) has happened since we last met.

I feel so bad about missing your 50th wedding anniversary party last year. I know that you were upset with us when we suddenly pulled out at the last minute.

We were all ready to come, Peter was going to collect us, but then Michael had a bad night and was too anxious about the journey.
He has completely lost his confidence or interest in going anywhere. Strange when you remember all those exotic holidays our families had together. Do you remember how Michael used to love driving up those steep mountain passes in Italy? God, didn't we curse him in the back, holding tightly on to the door handles going round those hairpin bends!

Michael doesn't drive anymore; they wouldn't renew his licence. For a while he felt it was a double humiliation, loss of his independence but also having to give control to me as the driver. I used to secretly moan to you about how he liked to be in control of everything, and I know you sometimes thought that I allowed him to be too dominant, but you knew it was easier for me to give in than to challenge him too much. No marriage is perfect, is it?

Now I think it would be a relief for him to take back control, or at least for us to have a proper conversation. Although, if I'm honest a small and unpleasant part of me takes pleasure in having the upper hand after all these years of not being able to express an opinion that was different to his. If I did, I'd perfected the art of pretending to listen when the inevitable lecture followed.

I look at him now, while he's sleeping in his chair in the living room or vacantly staring into space. I suppose it's ironic that as his mind empties, mine fills up with recollections of our lives together. I feel like I'm carrying memories for the both of us.

I confided in you that Michael was my first boyfriend (in fact my first friend) and I was so grateful that someone wanted me after leaving the Children's Home. Friendships were discouraged, as the nuns didn't want to deal with our sense of loss if someone we got close to went away. He promised to look after me and he has been true to his word. He was so determined to marry me, he would cycle miles from Hillingdon every evening to my lodgings in Harrow, and then back again, just so we could go for a walk together. Of course, he wasn't allowed into the lodgings and we had no money, so that was all we could do. I thought he was so kind and caring and could even cook and clean! I'd never heard of a man that could do that, although being brought up by the nuns, I don't know what men were supposed to do. (My only vague memories of men were of my father always being drunk before he finally left me in the home, so anything was going to be an improvement on that.) I suppose Michael's time in National Service gave him those domestic skills. He was ambitious too, talking about buying a house and setting up his own business.

Life's like a dream, isn't it? We dreamt it, and it happened, and when our sons took over the business Michael was so proud of what he and they had achieved.

Sometimes he asks Peter how business is, forgetting the company was sold a long time ago. But I know he takes comfort in still being able to use that phrase, 'how's business', an echo of when he was in his prime and the future was… well, just there was a future to look forward to. Looking back, business was always the dominant motivation in Michael's life, so I suppose it will be the last memory to fade.

Do you remember how Michael used to go out for lunch every day at work and when he retired he insisted I go with him? We used to laugh that he could be the most well informed restaurant critic in Hillingdon but I used to hate having to eat restaurant food when I was always trying to watch my weight. What irony, now it's me that has to help him get dressed and leave the house and since I've dropped four dress sizes I can happily eat a few more carbs. Of course, we can only go to the one restaurant now where they know him and he always has the same meal, but at least it's a change of scene for me and to see a few friendly faces to get me through the day. When one of the boys are with us they try and get him to use a knife and fork instead of a spoon but I think they are beginning to realise it's a losing battle. I suppose it's just him reverting back to a childlike state.

Conversation is almost impossible now, I think for Michael, the constant repetition of the same phrases is his way of anchoring himself to the world, whereas for me it's just a constant reminder of the world he no longer inhabits... It's got a lot worse these last few months and I know Peter was upset when Michael didn't recognise him the other day.

I suppose the most difficult thing for me to deal with is his relentless anxiety if he can't see me all the time. He's always calling for me if I'm out the room and tries to follow me, but he's so shaky on his feet now I'm worried that he'll have a fall so I have to constantly let him know where I am- even if I'm in the toilet! It's a bit like when the kids were young and we didn't get a moment's peace. The difference is we knew it was only for a short time and once they were sulky teenagers we'd look back with nostalgia about when they needed us. I try not to think too much about when Michael won't need me any more….

I promised myself I wouldn't sound self-pitying in this letter and it seems to have come out all wrong. Honestly, I'm so lucky to have had such a wonderful life and family and at least we don't have money worries.

Sally, give my love to James and the kids, it would be lovely to speak to you. The best time to phone would be around 11 a.m., Michael is usually asleep and quite calm then until lunch time.

Lots of love

Julia

P.S. Peter is in touch with your Amanda on Facebook and he tells me you've just come back from another cruise. He showed me the photos; looks like you had a great time. If you're going again, I've got loads of new outfits I bought for a cruise we had to cancel because Michael wasn't up to it. I keep meaning to give them away as they're far too big for me now. Anyway I wouldn't have an opportunity to wear them, but there are some pieces that might fit you.

Peter and Amanda   May 2018

Peter was into his second beer when he glanced up and saw her scanning the pub looking for him. He stood up and walked towards the bar with a welcoming grin, his arms outstretched. He was relieved he had already seen her photos on Facebook so his expression wouldn't register shock at her appearance.

'Amanda, at last! Sit down and I'll get us a drink, I've got a table by the window.
I can't believe we're finally in a pub together legally, I still have this ridiculous urge to show our fake I.D!'

As they relaxed into their chairs, drinks in hand, Amanda unconsciously ran her fingers through her once lustrous hair. Peter remembered how it used to shimmer around her, how she would then dip her head slightly and look up through her fringe. It used to have a very unsettling effect on him in those hormonally volatile days. Now it was a utilitarian grey crop that craved a stylish cut.

Amanda's face took on a nostalgic expression. 'That was another life, wasn't it? Of course, our kids create their fake IDs digitally now; you've got to admire their technical savvy. Mine are just coming up to Uni age, so God knows what they'll get up to when they're away from home.'

She paused, 'your sons must be a similar age - how are they, and of course, Lottie? You met her when you were at university didn't you- you must be one the few people I know still on their first marriage.'

Peter hesitated fractionally, spinning his beer glass between his hands.

'We're all good thanks, although the situation with my father is testing us somewhat. Lottie does resent how much time I have to spend with Mum to help her with Dad, and I'd be lying if I said it doesn't put a strain on our relationship. Of course, you know some of it because of the letter my Mum wrote your Mum. I'm glad she shared it with you and even happier that we're meeting, so good things can come from bad.'

Amanda noticed the worry lines etched into his face, thinking how like his father he was beginning to look. But it was a relief to be the confidante in someone else's story.

'It must be so hard for you all' she sympathised.

'Honestly, Amanda, you wouldn't recognise him. Do you remember when our families used to go on holiday together, we all used to be a bit wary of his temper?'

'Of course I do, remember that really embarrassing incident with the waiter who your Dad thought wasn't attentive enough?'

'God yes, and that was when he was relaxed on holiday, it was much worse when we were at home.

Well, now he sits in his chair as meek as a lamb. Mostly he forgets I'm there and after a while I just speak to Mum, but occasionally he gives me a beseeching look. I know there's something he wants to say but he can't grasp the thought and then it's gone.

Until recently he would repeat the same phrases, how he cycled to see Mum every day when they were courting, his time in the services and the places he was stationed, most of them in his imagination now, and he would ask me about business even though we sold the company years ago. It used to be so irritating although we'd try and humour him, but now he hardly says a word. I don't know what's worse. The other week he didn't even recognise me.'

Amanda listened intently. 'I suppose it's the stress that's caused your Mum to lose so much weight. She mentioned it in the letter.'

Peter smiled, 'I'm not surprised she mentioned it, she was always so conscious of her size compared to your Mum, I think there was a bit of competition there, don't you?'

He paused and smiled apologetically. 'Honestly, I don't want to make this all about me, I know how lucky I am to have both parents still around. I feel almost embarrassed talking about it compared to what you've been through.'

He was relieved he'd managed to broach the subject at last.

'I was so sorry to hear about your husband, he sounds like he was one of life's good guys. What a tribute to him that his work are paying for your kids to get through university, at least that must give you some solace.'

Amanda looked directly at Peter and her gaze momentarily made him relive those carefree teenage years. She dropped her eyes and inhaled sharply.

'Peter, I know you think I suggested we meet because of your troubles, but to be honest I needed to talk to you too, someone who's not part of my everyday life. I'm suffocated by people's kindness and although I know it's well intentioned I don't deserve it.'

Peter started to speak in what he hoped was a reassuring tone, 'Amanda you mustn't be so hard on yourself…..'

'No,' she interrupted, 'I have to say this. The truth is- and I can't admit this to anyone else- Brandon and I had a blazing row the night before the accident because he found out I'd been unfaithful. It was only once, when I was away at a conference and I immediately regretted it. But the guy kept texting me and Brandon must have sensed a change in my behaviour and got suspicious. He saw one of the texts before I had a chance to delete it. I'm tortured by the knowledge if he hadn't been so upset he would have been less preoccupied. He would have seen the car coming and had time to avoid it. When he was in the coma I kept telling myself that if only he would wake up I would do anything to make things right, but I suppose it's my penance that I have to live with this secret. Sometimes I want to scream at people to treat me as I really deserve, every sympathetic comment or gesture just creates more agony.

I even chopped my hair off and stopped wearing make up so that when I look in the mirror at least the reflection I see is stripped of the lies I have to armour myself with every day. People think my changed appearance is because of pure grief, but really it's my way of punishing myself for the consequences of my actions.'

Peter had remained completely silent, conscious that any interruption might stop the flow of her confession. Her brief animation dissipated as she slumped back into her chair.

"I'm so sorry, Amanda, he said as he leaned towards her and covered her small, shaking hand with his substantial one. 'It seems like we both have our troubles……'

About Michael   June 2018

Most people had a lucky number, but Michael had a lucky letter. H. He bought his first home with his new bride in Harrow, and started his business there. As success came, he moved his young family and business to Hillingdon. He even called his house Halcyon although Julia had raised an eyebrow at that one. If anyone asked him to describe his life, he would say 'Happy and Healthy'

Now as he sat in his chair staring out the window, the letter D had taken over.

D for Dementia. He couldn't articulate the word out loud but he knew people used to understand when he referred to 'his problem' and gesticulated in place of words. He'd watched his brother degenerate from a vibrant, witty man to an empty shell before he finally died in a dementia care home.

Michael used to wonder what was locked in his brother's mind in the later stages, was it a whirl of misfiring synapses, or was his aggression just a return to humanity's fundamental primal instincts? The disease had cruelly chosen to withhold his physical decline and in the early stages people would remark how 'well' his brother looked-that is, until his cognitive limitations became apparent and he would offend people with his no filter behaviour Now Michael sensed he had been sucked into that same netherworld. Sometimes a flutter of a thought would pass through his mind like a hovering butterfly. But just as he was about to grasp it, the recognition would fly away and, like the butterfly glittering so brilliantly and briefly, it would fade into oblivion. The thought degenerated into the ugly sister of a dying moth, beating its dark nocturnal wings futilely as it tried to enter his world.

He got scared looking in the mirror and wondered who that old man was in front of him looking so unkempt. Perhaps it was the enemy. He knew he'd get into trouble with the Sergeant for not being properly turned out and he'd probably end up on double guard duty. Trouble was, he can't find his uniform anywhere. Perhaps his mother had hidden it again to stop him going back to the barracks. She was always doing that; she would laugh and say she missed him so much when he was gone.

'Mum, where's the army stuff, I need it now!'

Julia walked into the room to find all the clothes in the drawers scattered on the floor. She'd forgotten to put the padlocks on them last night. Her knees were aching so much, but she'd have to get on the floor and put it all away.

'Love, it's me, your wife Julia. You're not in the army anymore, so you don't have to worry. But why don't you let me help you get dressed and comb your hair, you'd be good enough for inspection then, you'll be my smartest soldier in the regiment'.

Michael looked at Julia as a fragment of memory returned.

'Was Peter a soldier? A man came to see me last week, he said he was Peter but he wasn't wearing a uniform, so I think he was trying to trick me.'

Julia summoned all her reserves of patience as she looked bleakly into the days and weeks ahead. As she calmed Michael down and began the routine of dressing him for the day, she silently thanked the nuns in the Children's

Home. At least being lonely and unloved had made her resilient and taught her how to deal with the absence of hope.

Never had she needed it more.

By Hilary Lynch

Pass and Past
by Christina Barnatsos

Every redemptive score is as holy
As each guffaw, throwing back of the head -
Boast in academic accolades only,
I relate; retaliate back to bed.
My new home is a cistern of gold dust
Contained in matte-black, Thermos coffee cups.
Staring at faces that smile, they must,
I fumble my feet and try to look up.
Oh, London calls me, her lights on display
Attempting to pull me backwards again.
No warmth, no winter market, just the way
I left; alone, in beginnings of rain.

Here I am now in the midst of winter
Gold in my coffee, I do not miss her.

by Thomas Ryan

Contributors

John Donegan

Originally from Putney, John now lives in Eastcote and is a singer/songwriter. He has written over 300 songs and performed more than 1000 shows over the years – one of which being the first Hillingdon Literary Festival. He is currently writing an autobiography with the hope of turning it in to a musical. His current great interest is Bob Dylan, 1965-66.

James F McDermot

James grew up in West London and moved to Ascot in 1977 and has since had three separate careers: a theatrical agent; owning a sporting and social club; and advising private clients on investments. James has completed a Diploma in Creative Writing at Oxford University, mainly for the prose. The poetry added imagery to that prose, and the play-writing enhanced its dialogue. He also completed an MA at Brunel University London, under the tutelage of Professor Fay Weldon, concentrating on the novel, which remains work in progress.

Sola Janet Browne

Sola is an emerging Nigerian British writer of poetry and prose. She is a member of the Roundhouse Poetry Collective with whom she performed at Last Word Festival, Brainchild Festival and Citadel Festival 2018. She is also a writer for *Shout Out UK*, an online youth journalist platform and editor of *L.U.S.H. Talks*, an online publication she has dedicated to creative solutions for social and economic development in the BAME community. "To create new worlds, to document my existence and that of the people and things around me, to invoke feeling and thought but ultimately, I write poetry to inspire change."

Sarah Badhan

Sarah was born in the London Borough of Hillingdon in 1987 and attended Yeading Infant and Junior School from 1991-1998. After attending High School in neighbouring Northolt, she studied English Literature at Royal Holloway: University of London and graduated with a 2:1 BA Honours degree. Soon after graduating Sarah landed her first job working in book publishing as a Production Assistant, an industry that she has now been working in for a decade. Sarah's parents were raised in the Borough and her family have lived in Hillingdon for over fifty-five years.

Samuel Green

Sam is a Creative Writing graduate originally from South Wales. In his studies he specialised in screenwriting and poetry and was shortlisted for the Hillingdon Literary Festival 2017 Creative Writing Competition. He has self-published anthologies, working as both editor and writer for them, and performs his poetry at writing events. While studying at university he developed a dependence for coffee and cynicism and now lives out a cliché life as a struggling writer/waiter.

Neil Parker

Neil works at a mental health recovery centre in Harrow and lives in Hillingdon. As part of his current job, he runs a creative writing group for clients and remarks that 'it is amazing to support the wonderfully talented and creative individuals I work with'. He has a long-standing fascination with fantasy and sci-fi fiction, since his school days in the early eighties, playing roleplaying games and reading Lord of the Rings and is now endeavouring to write a novel.

Michelle Stevens

Michelle is a Hillingdon resident who moved back to the area after university a few years ago, which helped inspire the text which tackles issues including London housing, graduate jobs, mental health and homelessness. One hears a lot on the news about homelessness as a crisis in London, and, often, assumptions are made about their pasts; so when Michelle read an article about a man - a graduate – whose life had spiralled into tragedy resulting in homelessness, it was scary to see how relatable the man's journey was, and that really resonated with her.

Jonathan Pizarro

Jonathan Pizarro has recently completed a BA in English & Creative Writing at Brunel University London, graduating with a first-class degree, and awarded the Arthur Scott prize for his Creative Writing dissertation. He contributed to and co-edited the Brunel third year Creative Writing anthology: *Totem*. Jonathan has contributed fiction, poetry, and journalistic pieces to various small-press and online magazines. As a Gibraltarian, he is interested in bringing his cultural heritage to the centre of his narrative work, as well as exploring ideas around language, colonialism, and borders. Jonathan lives in London with his husband, and a lot of books.

Hilary Lynch

Hilary grew up in a small town on the outskirts of Glasgow in the 1970s, attended a local comprehensive school and was the first and only member of her family to attend university. After graduating with a degree in Chemistry in the late 80s, Hilary moved to London and worked as a Research Assistant at University College London. By the mid '90s she had obtained a Ph.D. in Biotechnology at Surrey University and then became an academic at Reading University. Hilary enjoys drawing and painting, restoring period properties and yoga. She currently lives in Windsor with her husband and three children and works in Research Development at Brunel University London.

Angela Narayn

Angela has lived in the Borough for most of her life and remarks that she has witnessed many changes. These include the increasing diversity of ethnicity and its cultural impact and the urban growth and development and the resulting environmental concerns. She is interested in writing and literature and how the power of the written word can transform and enrich the human experience. Angela is a member of the Ruislip Writers' group.

Chris Miller

Chris describes himself as a "lapsed creative writer", having started experimenting during his English Literature degree in 2002. In 2018 he took a creative writing class with (the wonderful) Emma Filtness and it got him back into the mood. He has been dabbling since. Chris remarks that he wrote this piece "during a rare afternoon off work based upon some experiences from starting an allotment. Allotments and the community surrounding them are inspirational in so many different ways!".

Jordan Friend

Jordan wishes to write for everyone, and focuses on topics underrepresented in the main stream media, whilst not shying away from the explicit or troubling. In Friend's latest collection, 'This is Necessary', written for his dissertation, he wrote from his and his close friend's personal experiences. Removing all mention of gender where possible, and talking on difficult subjects such as exploring his own sexuality and mental health issues. Being a writer of poetry first and prose second, Friend's style is largely moulded around punchy images and a strong sense of rhythm. Jordan truly hopes you enjoy his work.

Andy Lewis

Andy Lewis is a 22-year-old writer, in his third year at the University of Roehampton, where he studies Creative Writing. He was born and raised in Hillingdon, and is still living there now. He usually writes poems, short stories and screenplays, but is currently working on a novel too. He has had poems published in two anthologies, *Candlelit Thoughts: A Collection Of Poetry*, and *Everlasting Love: A Collection Of Poetry*. In 2016, he was shortlisted for Hillingdon Literary Festival's *Writing Local Thinking Global* award for his short story *The Witch's House*.

Vivienne Burgess

Vivienne is a young writer based between London and the North East of England. She graduated from Brunel University London with a First in English with Creative Writing and has lived and worked in Hillingdon for the past five years. Her work has been published by *LossLit*, *365tomorrows* and *The Nottingham Review*. Vivienne volunteers for Cats Protection and the RSPCA and is currently looking for her first full-time role in the editorial/publishing industry.

Eden Kofi Joseph

Eden Kofi Joseph is a songwriter and rapper from West Drayton, Hillingdon. He is of Mixed African Caribbean and European heritage, and has been in and out of the family home since age – moving around the cultural melting pot that is London. His latest work focuses on his colourful experience growing up, absorbing different cultures, mannerisms and attitudes. Not least the 'masculine experience', what it takes to be 'a man' in 2018 and how this effects our brothers, mothers and sisters.

Jake Horowitz

Jake Horowitz is a Canadian writer who has found a second home in Hillingdon. He previously worked as a TV writer in Toronto, Canada, but since coming to England has branched out into writing in other formats. He first came to London to get a Masters in Creative Writing at the University of Roehampton, where he wrote his story *Leo and Cole*, among other stories which he has since had published internationally. He is currently working on his feature film debut, *Who You Know*.

Simon Engwell

Simon Engwell is an engineer and management consultant who lives in the Borough of Hillingdon. He is a Street Pastor: caring, helping and listening to people on the streets of outer London late at night. He is interested in people of all different backgrounds and circumstances in life. His poetry often draws on the circumstances of people shopping, living and playing on the streets of London.

Russell Christie

A mature student, currently studying at Brunel University London, Russell has a long, dilatory writing career, beginning with travel journalism in the late 1990s, published in *The Pink Paper* and *Gay Times*, and short stories published in San Francisco in *The Bay Area Purveyor*. Not finding much financial success in producing gay themed literature, he became a global wanderer. He has lived in several, developing countries while teaching English, finding the dynamic of social, ideological and economic change both challenging and stimulating. He published his first novel, *The Queer Diary of Mordred Vienna*, in 2015.

Taiwo Oyenola

25 years old and originally from Nigeria, but born and raised in London, Taiwo graduated from Brunel University London and has recently completed a PGCE course in primary education at Brunel. His goal in life is to excel in academia and his profession, to try to inspire people to help those who are suffering and to empower people to reach their full potential. Taiwo writes poetry as a means to raise awareness of issues and hopefully bring change.

Matthew Healing

Matthew Healing is a North-London born writer, poet, and journalist. After finishing A-levels in Edmonton, he spent three years at Brunel University London studying Creative Writing. During his time in Uxbridge, he produced a novella, over forty short stories, two screenplays, and three collections of poetry. Hillingdon was a major inspiration for Matthew, particularly while studying Psychogeography, where he partook in, and conducted, numerous unplanned walks around the Borough. He is currently living in Edmonton, publishing content from his time at university, and freelancing as both a cultural and sports journalist.

Macauley Raymond Foster

Macauley is an MA student at Brunel University London who's been writing for fun before he realised it was a job. A keen magician, in his spare time he enjoys thinking of pretentious words for illusionist and aspires to perform at Covent Garden. When not writing, performing or waiting for Doors of Stone, Mac enjoys playing Dungeons and Dragons as an excuse to do stupid voices, escaping from responsibilities inside fat fantasy novels, pretending he can draw, juggling, cultivating an out of hand fountain pen collection and referring to himself in the third person.

Mark O'Loughlin

Mark has completed a number of writing courses at Birkbeck, City Lit and most recently at the Faber Academy and has written a novel (*Dad Died in Vegas*) as well as short stories. He was delighted that two of his poems were selected for publication in the

Hillingdon Literary Festival 2017 anthology as he has been a Hillingdon resident since 2003.

Lia Courtenay Harlin

Lia is a BA Theatre and Creative Writing graduate of Brunel University London and a recent graduate in MA Music Theatre at The Royal Central School of Speech and Drama. Lia jokes that she should have been working on her Masters final project but this competition was the perfect procrastination and gave her a chance to write about something she wanted to, rather than something she had to! Further stating that "after nineteen years of full time education it is finally time to face my fears and step into the real world, pen at the ready".

Connor Smith

Connor is a 20-year-old Creative Writing student at Brunel University London. Originally from North Hertfordshire, he has spent the past two years living in Uxbridge. Connor stated that throughout his Literary education, he never found a fondness for poetry until being introduced to more contemporary styles of writing. His aim is therefore to write poetry that appeals to people who may struggle to find a connection with more classical styles of poetry. This includes finding a more accessible style of poetry, utilising comedy and conversational-style language that is intertwined with a poem's meaning.

Adam Johnson

Adam recently graduated Brunel University London with a First Honours in Theatre and Creative Writing, he has since returned home to Kent county though he thinks of Uxbridge fondly and often. He is caught in that terrible moment in time all students face after leaving education, figuring out what to do next. However, the future looks bright. Adam has recently finished a tour of his co-written musical Super Hero with the National Youth Music Theatre. In the meantime, he enjoys reading and catching up with uni friends scattered across the country.

Vivien Brown

Vivien Brown writes commercial women's fiction, including almost 150 women's magazine short stories and two successful novels, all with domestic, romantic or dramatic themes. She has also written many articles on her specialist topic of working and reading with the under-fives, and a book about cryptic crosswords. Vivien is a fellow of the *Society of Women Writers and Journalists*, the UK's oldest society for professional female writers, looking after their social media accounts and administering their competitions programme. She lives in Uxbridge with her husband and cats, loves TV soaps and quizzes and is a proud grandmother of two.

Aisling Lally

Aisling, aged 19, is a keen playwright and poet. She is currently studying English Literature and History at the University of York. Initially training as an actress at Tring Park School for the Performing Arts and the Oxford School of Drama, as well as working with the National Youth Film Academy and the Youth Music Theatre UK, storytelling both in writing and performing has played a vital role in her teenage years. It's a huge passion of Aisling's and is something she hopes to continue for years to come.

Luke Buffini

Luke is a 26 year old living in Ruislip where he has lived all his life. He states that his experience of living in Hillingdon has always been one of being on the outside: where things are quiet, slow and anonymous; and looking in: where everything is happening. His writing reflects this. Recently, he has travelled in Europe and worked in Hayes as a postman. He loves playing football and exploring the treasure trove of bars and restaurants in London.

Iris Hontiveros Mauricio

Originally from the Philippines, Iris is pursuing a Masters in Creative Writing in Brunel University London. While not particularly devout herself, most of her writing bears strong influences of her Roman Catholic upbringing, along with themes of history, mythology, pop culture and the arts—things from which she draws much inspiration. When she isn't busy wrestling her muses and challenging her creativity, Iris can be found living a sedentary life similar to that of a feline's: eating, limited socializing, succumbing to bouts of lethargy when caught in warm patches of sunlight, and binge-watching shows and films.

Lorraine Collins

Lorraine life so far has been working, enjoying family and friends and making the most of good times. Now retired, she is also looking forward to new experiences, including travelling in a newly acquired campervan. Lorraine always wanted to write fiction and now has the opportunity and time to see, as she says, "if anything she writes is worth reading. This competition will be the first time I've dipped my toes in literary waters and take the first scary steps to sharing my work. Hope the sharks don't get me!"

Christina Barnatsos

Christina is a 22-year-old Hillingdon resident. She studied English at the University of Nottingham and is a keen vocalist and instrumentalist who plays the drums, piano and guitar. She is enamoured by nature and loves to converse with friends and strangers alike. Her favourite writers include C.S Lewis and T.S Eliot. Her focus is primarily on taking fictitious situations and bringing them to life through her writing, they can be mundane or fantastical, but she loves the idea of getting into the lives of others and living out the ordinary through a different lens.